Alfred Bagby

Adverbs in Horace and Juvenal

Alfred Bagby

Adverbs in Horace and Juvenal

ISBN/EAN: 9783337367114

Printed in Europe, USA, Canada, Australia, Japan

Cover: Foto ©Andreas Hilbeck / pixelio.de

More available books at **www.hansebooks.com**

ADVERBS

IN

HORACE AND JUVENAL.

A DISSERTATION

PRESENTED TO THE JOHNS HOPKINS UNIVERSITY FOR THE DEGREE OF
DOCTOR OF PHILOSOPHY.

BY

ALFRED BAGBY, Jr.,

OF VIRGINIA.

...

BALTIMORE:
1891.

CONTENTS.

For Horace: Index of Zangemeister (Bentley's Horace, II; Berlin, 1869); Dictionary of Koch; editions of the Satires, of Fritzsche (Leipsic, 1875), Schütz (Berlin, 1881), Palmer (London, 1883), Kiessling (Berlin, 1886), Orelli (Berlin, 1890); editions of the Epistles, of Schütz (Berlin, 1883), Wilkins (London, 1885), Kiessling (Berlin, 1889); dissertations of Waltz, *Langue et Métrique d'Horace* (Paris, 1881); Beste, *De generis dicendi inter Horatii carmina sermonesque discrimine* (Münster, 1876); Brand, *Intersitne aliquid inter Q. Horatii Flacci satiras et eiusdem epistolas, et quid id sit, quaeritur* (Czernowitz, 1874).

For Juvenal: Jahn's Index (Jahn's Juvenal, Berlin, 1851); editions of Mayor (London, 1886), Jahn-Buecheler (Berlin, 1886), Weidner (Leipsic, 1889); dissertation of Weise, *Vindiciae Iuvenalianae* (Halle, 1884).

General: Lexica of Harper, White and Riddle, Forcellini, and Klotz; indices to all the Latin authors of Lemaire's *Bibliotheca Classica Latina* (in this series the indices to Plautus, Terence, Pliny the Elder, Juvenal appear to be well-nigh complete, those to other authors more or less defective); Merquet's Lexica to Cicero's Orations and to Caesar; Koch's Dictionaries to Nepos and Vergil; Burmann's Index to Ovid, Friedlander's to Martial (Friedlander's Martial, Leipsic, 1886); Gerber and Greef's Lexicon to Tacitus (first nine fascicles). Some fifteen other indices to minor authors.

Dr. = Draeger's *Historische Syntax der Lateinischen Sprache* (Leipsic, 1878). Neue = Neue's *Formenlehre der Lateinischen Sprache* (Berlin, 1877). Reisig = Reisig's *Lateinische Sprachwissenschaft* (Schmalz and Landgraf, Berlin, 1888). Krebs = Krebs' *Antibarbarus der Lateinischen Sprache* (Basel, 1888). Hand = Hand's *Tursellinus* (Leipsic, 1829). Archiv = *Archiv für Lateinische Lexicographie und Grammatik.*

A COMPARATIVE STUDY OF THE ADVERBS OF HORACE AND JUVENAL.

INTRODUCTION.

It is the object of this paper to show, in a comparative way, the use of adverbs in the Satires and Epistles of Horace and in Juvenal, and to discuss the various uses of the words singly when such treatment seems desirable. I shall first compare the adverbs as to form and then as to syntax.

The diction and syntax of the Satires and Epistles of Horace offer peculiar difficulties. The language is not that of prose, nor of poetry, nor yet of common life, but a blending of all three. Juvenal's style in turn, while in general nearer the prose norm than that of the average poet, yet at times presents exceedingly unusual positions and constructions. The rhetorical element, too, must be considered constantly.

As regards the vocabulary, it will be found that Horace is much broader than the later satirist, using many adverbs not occurring in Juvenal, whereas the latter employs comparatively few not found in Horace. This is due mainly to two reasons. First, Horace is much freer in the use of rare words, and not infrequently coins new adverbs to suit his purpose. Again, the prose[1] and vulgar element, more especially in the Satires,[2] in Horace allows words not to be found in poetical or urbane diction. As regards also the number of times the single words occur, Horace's use is larger than that of Juvenal in almost every class of adverbs. Certain adverbs of place are a noteworthy exception—due to the free use of these words by Juvenal to express time and other relations. This usage is commonly in keeping with the general post-Augustan development.

---

[1] Horace S. I. 4[11] neque si qui scribat uti nos *sermoni propriora*, putes hunc esse poetam.

[2] As regards the difference in the diction of the Satires and Epistles consult Brand, *Intersitne aliquid inter Q. Horatii Flacci satiras et eiusdem epistolas, et quid id sit, quaeritur* (Czernowitz, 1874).

As far as the syntax of the two authors appears from their use of adverbs, as would naturally be expected, Juvenal is much further removed from the classical prose norm than Horace.

In the course of this comparison surprising differences will be seen in the vocabularies of the two authors in the case of some common words. Thus, *eo* occurs 9 times in Horace, not once in Juvenal; *simul* and *frustra* 27 and 8 times, respectively, in Horace, not once in Juvenal; *ita, qui, nimis, tum* 23, 15, 6, 15 times, respectively, in Horace, and 4, 0, 1, 3 times, respectively, in Juvenal.

To the contrary, *tunc, inde, illic, quotiens, pariter, ibi* occur 34, 40, 17, 19, 11, 7 times, respectively, in Juvenal, and 3, 8, 4, 3, 4, 0 times in Horace. Where such a difference exists, I have made an effort to find a substitute of the author using the word the smaller number of times, and why the adverb was avoided, if it was avoided. In the case of several words this effort has been fruitless. Why does Juvenal not use *frustra, simul, nimium*? What does he use instead of *frustra, nimium, qui, prope*? Why does Horace totally avoid *ibi*? What does he use instead of *ibi* and *illic*?

In the Satires and Epistles of Horace there are 4071 verses, in Juvenal 3840 verses. The proportion, then, is nearly as 25 : 24.

I.—As to Form.

1. *Adverbs in* -tim *and* -sim.

In consideration of the period of the two authors, these adverbs would be expected to be more numerous in H. than in J. (Dr. I 117), but H. uses 11 occurring 18 times, J. 2 occurring 5 times. H. uses: *certatim* once, *confestim* once, *furtim* 5 times, *passim* twice, *paulatim* twice, *praesertim* twice, *raptim* once, *singultim* once, *tribulim* once, *vicissim* once, *viritim* once.

J. uses: *paulatim* 4 times, *praesertim* once. I find no reason for J.'s avoiding *furtim, passim, raptim*, if he did avoid them. These words occur in contemporary poets. *Certatim* and *confestim*[1] I find in silver poetry only Luc. 4⁴³⁴ and 4³¹². *Singultim* appears first H. S. 1. 6⁵⁶, and not again until Appuleius. *Tribulim* S. 2. 1⁶⁹ is ἅπαξ λεγόμενον in poetry. *Viritim* Ep. 2. 1⁹² occurs elsewhere in poetry only in Plautus and Lucr. 2¹¹⁷³.

---

[1] *Confestim*, occurring several times in Lucretius and Catullus, is rare in the Augustan poets. H. Ep. 1. 12⁹, Verg. A. 9²³¹.

2. *Adverbs in* -um.

Of this class of adverbs H. uses 18 occurring 109 times, J. 16 occurring 60 times.[1] These forms are in their origin adverbial accusatives. They have, however, the force of adverbs and are to be regarded as such.[2] The usage is by no means foreign to English, in which language it is poetical and vulgar.[3]

H. uses: *aculum.* S. 1. 3[26] cur . . . tam cernis *aculum.* 8[11]. This word, found several times in Plautus, occurs twice in Terence, Cic. Phil. 12. 11. 26, Verg. A. 9[254], Livy 29. 14. 5. *aeternum.* Ep. 1. 10[11] serviet *aeternum.* This word occurs in Vergil 5 times, Ovid T. 5. 3[41], M. 6[369], Tac. An. 3. 26, 12. 28, Suet. Tib. 34, and in Statius and Sidonius. *certum.* S. 2. 5[109] *certum* vigilans. Cf. Ovid Her. 10[9] *incertum* vigilans. S. 2. 6[27]. *decorum.* Ep. 1. 7[27] dulce loqui . . . ridere *decorum.* This word appears to be ἅπαξ λεγόμενον here. *indoctum.* Ep. 2. 2[9] canet *indoctum.*

longum. A. P. 459 'succurrite' longum clamet, 'io cives,' i. e. so as to be heard from afar. Wilkins compares μακρὸν ἄϋσεν Hom. Il. Γ 81.

In *J.*: *aestivum.* 14[295] *aestivum* tonat. *altum.* 1[16] *altum* dormiret. *horrendum.* 6[185] intonet *horrendum.* *longum.* 6[65] *longum* attendit. This adverb occurs Plaut. Ep. 3. 2[40], Ps. 2. 3[31], Verg. A. 10[740], Ov. M. 5[65], Stat. Th. 7[500], 10[467].

rectum. 3[107] si *rectum* minxit amicus.[4]

3. *Adverbs in* -orsum.

In *H.*: *dextrorsum.* S. 2. 3[50] *dextrorsum* abit. *introrsum.* S. 2. 1[65] *introrsum* turpis. Ep. 1. 16[45]. *quorsum*—5 times. *retrorsum.* Ep. 1. 1[75], 18[88], ne mutata *retrorsum* te ferat aura. *sinistrorsum.* S. 2. 3[50].

J. uses no word of this termination.[5]

The comparative frequency of the occurrence of words of this ending in Plautus, their small use by Cicero and the almost

[1] Only such words are treated below as appear to need comment, because of their being rare.
[2] Notice H. S. 2. 6[27] clare *certumque* locuto. If *multum* and *nimium* have the force of adverbs, these words have.
[3] Cf. "*monstrous* wise," "*swift* swimming space," and similar expressions.
[4] For a full discussion of this class of adverbs in Latin consult Reisig N. 555.
[5] *Prorsus, rursum* and *rursus* are not counted—the ending being no longer felt in the case of those words.

entire absence of them from his Orations, and their rarity in the best poetry[1] point to their origin in the *sermo vulgaris*.

4. *Adverbs in'*-cumque.

H. uses: *quacumque* S. 1. 6$^{31,\ 111}$. ·
quandocumque S. 1. 9^{33}, Ep. 1. 14$^{1\tau}$, 16^{58}.
quocumque S. 2. 4^{89}, Ep. 1. 1^{13}, A. P. 100.
ubicumque S. 1. 2^{62}, Ep. 1. 3^{34}.
J. uses: *quocumque* 14^{277}. *ubicumque* 4^{35}. *utcumque* 10^{271}.

Where *quandocumque* might have been employed J. uses a) *si quando* 3^{173} ipsa . . . colitur *si quando* theatro maiestas. 12^{23}.

b) *quotiens* 2^{136} Curius quid sentit . . . *quotiens* hinc talis ad illos umbra venit? 3$^{10,\ 270,\ 306,\ 318}$, 5$^{28,\ 145}$, 6$^{67,\ 180,\ 535,\ 642}$, 7^{179}, 9$^{51,\ 111}$, 10^{23}, 14^{21}.

5. *Adverbs in* -ter.[2]

Of these H. uses 25 occurring 43 times; J. but 10 occurring 23 times.

The following not used by H. occur in J.: *breviter, civiliter, graviter, populariter, violenter*. *Populariter* (3^{37}) occurs five times in Cicero. The only example I find elsewhere is Quint. 12. 9. 2.

Not used by J. and occurring in H. are: *acriter, amabiliter, communiter, constanter, convenienter, decenter, fideliter, frugaliter, inaniter, inpariter, insolabiter, largiter, leniter, leviter, loquaciter, mediocriter, patienter, prodigialiter, socialiter, verniliter*, and *viriliter*.

It will be noted that of these 19 words 14 are of more than 3 syllables. The use of these long, and in most cases rare, adverbs is one of the characteristics of the style of the Epistles of H. With the exception of *frugaliter*,[3] *communiter*,[4] and *verniliter*,[5] they are confined to the Epistles; and, excepting *communiter* and *patienter*, occur but once.[6]

---

[1] In the poets from Catullus to Juvenal I find only H. Od. 1. 34^3, 4. 8^{16}, Epod. 9^{20}, Verg. A. 3^{690}, Ov. M. 13^{338}, F. 4^{445}, Pers. 5^5, Luc. 9^{652}, Val. 3^{268}.

[2] H. Osthoff (Archiv IV, pp. 455–466, reported in the *American Journal of Philology* X, pp. 484–485) holds these adverbs to be derived from the corresponding adjective + *iter*. Cf. our *straightway*.

[3] S. 1. 4^{107}.   [4] Epod. 16^{15}, Ep. 1. 2^{13}.   [5] S. 2. 6^{108}.

[6] I note also the frequency with which adjectives in -*ilis* and -*abilis* occur in the Ep. Thus 1. 2^{22} *immersabilis*, 2^{43} *volubilis*, 18^{71} *inrevocabilis*, 19^{17}, 20^{25}, 2. 1^{100}, 2$^{132,\ 179}$, A. P. 121, 123, 206, 368, 408. Cf. Waltz, *Langue et Métrique d'Horace*, p. 67.

Inpariter, insolabiliter, and *socialiter* were coined by H., and are ἅπαξ λεγόμενα—see Kiessling on Ep. 1. 14⁸ and A. P. 75, Schütz on A. P. 75 and 258, and Dr. I 112. *Insolabiliter* is a bold formation. *Potenter* (A. P. 40) is ἅπαξ λεγόμενον in the sense of that passage, and is a very rare word (H. Odes 3. 16⁹, Quint. 12. 10⁷², Val. Max. 1. 1. 1). This word appears to have been coined by H., as was also *prodigialiter,* another rare word. *Verniliter* S. 2. 6¹⁰⁸ appears to be ἅπαξ λεγόμενον in the sense in which it is there used, and is rare.

From the above it is seen that there is a broad difference between H. and J. in their use of adverbs in *-ter.* The statement as to the vocabularies (p. 2) is illustrated.

6. *Adverbs in* ē *and* ĕ.

The proportion of these adverbs in H. and J.—both as to the number of words used and the frequency of their occurrence—is nearly as 3 is to 2.

In *H.:*¹ *damnose* S. 2. 8³⁴, *gelide* A. P. 171, *laeve* Ep. 1. 7⁵² are ἅπαξ λεγόμενα. *Sinistre* A. P. 452 appears to have been first used by H.

In *J.: here* 3²¹.² This form is used by Plautus, Cicero, Horace, Ovid, Seneca, and Martial—who employs it 5 times, *heri* twice.³ Quint 1. 7. 22 : *Here* nunc e littera terminamus. H. uses *here* S. 2. 8². Neither H. nor J. uses *heri. ferme* 8⁷³, 13²³⁶. *Ferme* appears in all periods of the language. It is entirely avoided by Caesar, Nepos, and Cicero in the Orations. Sallust uses it once. Livy and Velleius are very fond of *ferme.* Curtius uses it 4. 5. 1, 9. 8. 30, and elsewhere, Pliny the Elder 2. 39. 106. Tacitus uses *ferme* 28 times, *fere* but 5 times. *Ferme* is not found in the *Dialogus*—in which work *fere* occurs 4 times.⁴ Schmalz states that *ferme* was a favorite word with the late writers.⁵ In poetry I find *ferme* only in Plautus and Terence, Lucr. 3⁶⁵, and J. 8⁷³, 13²³⁶.

¹ Only such words are mentioned below as appear to need comment.
² Priscian 15. 3. 14. 1011 recognizes the form *here* here.
³ For examples and further information see Neue II, p. 685.
⁴ *Lexicon Taciteum* of Gerber and Greef, p. 456. Draeger, however, holds that *fere* occurs in Tacitus only once—*Dialogus* 16. See his *Syntax und Sti des Tacitus,* p. 9.
⁵ Müller's *Handbuch der klassi. Altertumswissenschaft,* II, p. 554.

6

7. *Adverbs in* ō *and* ŏ.

The proportion of this class of adverbs in H. and J. is as 3 is
to 2, as regards the number of words used, and nearly the same
as to the number of times the words occur. No word of this
termination needs comment.

8. *Adverbs in* -tenus.[1]

H. uses: *hactenus* S. 1. 2^{123}, 4^{63}. *quadam . . . tenus* Ep. 1.
1^{32}. *quatenus* S. 1. 1^{64}, 3^{76}, 2. 4^{57}. *Quadamtenus* is used by Pliny
the Elder and Gellius (Dr. I 127). Other examples of tmesis in
H. are: *inque vicem* S. 1. 3^{111},[2] *quo . . . cumque* Ep. 1. 1^{15}, *quo . . .
circa* S. 2. 6^{65}.

J. uses only *quatenus* 12^{102}.

9. *Adverbs with prepositional prefix.*

H. uses: *abhinc* Ep. 2. 1^{36}. *dehinc* S. 1. 3^{101}, A. P. 144.
deinde S. 1. 5^{77}, 6^{119}, 2. 8^{75}. *insuper* S. 2. 4^{68}. *in . . . vicem* S.
1. 3^{141}. *protinus* S. 2. 5^{21}, Ep. 1. 12`, 18^{67}. *posthac* S. 1, 1^{21}, 2.
2^{107}, 3^{297}.

postmodo S. 2. 6^{27}. *subinde* S. 2. 5^{103}, Ep. 1. 8^{15}.

Abhinc appears to be a prose word. I find no other example
in poetry except those in Plautus, Terence, Lucr. 3^{967}, and Pacuv.
apud Caris. 2, p. 175. *Postmodo*,[3] used by H. Odes 1. 28^{31},
avoided by Vergil, and a favorite word with Ovid, appears not to
occur in silver poetry. *Subinde* S. 2. 5^{103}, Ep. 1. 8^{15} appears to be
used first by H. and Livy.[4]

J. uses *deinde*—12 times. *posthac* 7^{16}, 8^{7}, 14^{15}. *protinus*—7
times.

10. *Prepositional Adverbs.*

H. uses: *ante* S. 1. 1^{37}, 2. 3^{135}. *circum* S. 2. 8^{7}. *contra*—9
times.

extra Ep. 2. 1^{31}. *insuper* S. 2. 4^{68}.
intra Ep. 2. 1^{31}.[5] *post*—8 times.

---

[1] *Protinus* is not included.
[2] Tmesis in this word is common in the poets.
[3] Schmalz, *Ueber den Sprachgebrauch des Asinius Pollio*, p. 42.
[4] Dr. I 126, Wilkins to H. Ep. 1. 8^{15}.
[5] Bentley's emendation Ep. 2. 1^{31} from *nil intra est oleam* to *nil intra est olea*
now finds general acceptation.

super S. 1. 2⁶⁵, 2. 7⁷ˣ, Ep. 2. 2³³. *supra* Ep. 2. 2¹⁶⁵. *ultra*—6 times.

I find no other example of *extra* or *intra* used adverbially in poetry except Ovid F. 6¹⁹¹—*extra*. Cicero does not use *extra* adverbially in his Orations. Nepos does not use it ; Caesar only B. C. 3. 69. 4. *Intra* is very rare until post-Augustan times. It occurs, however, in Sallust, and *Bellum Hispaniense* 35.

J. uses : *ante*—9 times. *contra*—6 times. *infra* 3²⁰⁴. *post* 6⁵⁰⁴. *ultra*—5 times.

H. uses of this class 10 adverbs occurring 30 times, J. 5 occurring 22 times.

11. *Other Adverbs.*

Auctius H. S. 2. 6⁵ is ἅπαξ λεγόμενον. *dulce* H. Ep. 1. 7³⁷, 2. 2⁹. Cf. *grande, suave,* and *triste* below. This poetical use of neuter adjectives in *e* as adverbs seems to have had its origin with Catullus (51⁵, 61⁷), and is most probably a Graecism. J. has only one example of this usage, which occurs not infrequently in Statius. For its range in Latin consult Neue (Berlin, 1890) II 591–2. *grande* (J. 6³¹⁷) occurs elsewhere Ovid Rem. Am. 375, Pers. 5⁷, Stat. Th. 12⁶ˣ⁴, S. 3. 1⁵⁰, ¹·¹⁰. Cf. *dulce* above. *perraro* H. S. 2. 5⁵⁰ and *persaepe* H. S. 1. 2ˣ², 3¹⁰, A. P. 349 are prose words. Where *persaepe* might have been employed, J. uses *saepius* 6⁵³⁷.

quandoquidem (J. 1¹¹², 10¹⁴⁶, 13¹²⁹) is not found in H. *suave* H. S. 1. 4⁷⁶. Cf. *dulce* above. *triste* H. S. 1. 8⁴¹. Cf. *dulce* and *suave* above. *ubivis* H. S. 1. 4⁷⁴. I find this word elsewhere only in Terence and Cicero.

II.—As to Use.

1. *Adverbs of Place.*

alio, H. 2,[1] J. o. S. 2. 1³² usquam decurrens *alio.* 2⁵⁵ nam frustra vitium vitaveris illud, si te *alio* pravum detorseris.

eo, H. 9, J. o. a) *Thither.* Ep. 2. 2¹⁰ ibit *eo* quo vis. b) *To that degree, to such a point.* Ep. 2. 1¹²⁶ *eo* rem venturam ut . . . c) *Causal.* S. 1. 1³⁶, 3³⁰ rideri . . . *eo* quod . . . toga defluit. 9⁵⁵, 2. 3¹²⁰ *eo* quod. A. P. 222. For this use of *eo* see under *inde*, p. 42.

Eo is a prose word. I find no example in poetry except those in Plautus, Terence, and the S. and Ep. of H. Instead of *eo* causal, J. uses *hinc* and *inde*. See under *hinc* c) and *inde* a).

---

[1] "H. 2" means that *alio* occurs twice in the S. and Ep. of H.

foras, H. 2, J. o.   Ep. 1. 5²⁵ ne fidos inter amicos sit qui dicta *foras* eliminet. 7³¹.

foris, H. 2, J. 2.   In *H.:* S. 1. 10³⁰ patriis intermiscere petita verba *foris.*   Schütz states, in his note on this passage, that *foris* in this sense, "from without, from abroad," is found in Plautus often.   It occurs Lucr. 4¹⁰³², 5⁵⁴³, 6¹⁹, Cic. Or. 2. 39. 163, 2. 40. 173, Inv. 1. 11. 15, Tusc. 3. 3. 6, Nep. Dion 9. 6.   *A foris* occurs Pliny 17. 24. 227.

hac H. 2, J. o.   S. 2. 2⁶⁴ *hac* urget lupus, *hac* canis.   Ep. 2. 2⁷⁵ *hac* fugit canis, *hac* ruit sus.   In post-Augustan Latin I find *hac* only Phaedr. Fab. Nov. 27. 8, Pliny Ep. 2. 17. 18, 5. 6. 19, and Stat. Th. 6²²¹.¹   Instead of *hac* . . . *hac* J. uses *illinc* . . . *hinc, inde* . . . *hinc.*   See under *hinc* in J. e).

hic, H. 17, J. 25.   In *H.:* a) *Of time,* "*here,*" "*at this point.*" S. 1. 9⁷ *hic* ego, 'pluris hoc,' inquam, 'mihi eris.'   9²⁶, 2. 8¹⁶.² b) *In this, in this thing.*   S. 1. 10ˢ et est quaedam tamen *hic* quoque virtus.   c) *ubi* . . . *hic.*   S. 2. 3²²¹ ergo ubi prava stul-titia, *hic* summa est insania.

In *J.:* a) *Here, at this point (of time),* a) *above.*   1¹⁵⁰ dices *hic* forsitan 'unde . . .'   15⁴ *hic* gaudere libet quod non viola-verit ignem.   b) *Among them.*   2¹¹⁰, ¹¹¹ *hic* nullus verbis pudor . . ., *hic* turpis Cybeles . . . libertas.   c) *In anaphora.*   2¹¹⁰, ¹¹¹.

hinc, H. 14, J. 19.   In *H.:* a) With *pendere.*   S. 1. 4⁶ *hinc* omnis pendet Lucilius.   Hand quotes Varro R. R. 3. 1. 10 de quibus exponendis initium capiam *hinc.*   Cf. Schütz on S. 1. 4⁶. b) *From this, from these.*   S. 1. 2⁷⁹ nihil *hinc* diffindere possum. 2. 2¹²⁷ quantum *hinc* imminnet?, i. e. from my possessions.   A. P. 318.   c) *Of cause, source.*   Ep. 1. 19⁴¹ *hinc* illae lachrimae.   This passage being a quotation, it may be said that H. avoids this usage.   d) =*tum, postea.*   S. 1. 9⁴⁴ 'Maecenas quomodo tecum?' *hinc* repetit.   *Hinc* in this sense occurs Pers. 3¹⁰³, and in Pliny the Elder, Tacitus, and other silver writers.

In *J.:* a) *For ex his.*   15⁷⁷ labitur *hinc* quidam.   b) *From this,* b) *above.*   7¹¹³ veram deprendere messem si libet, *hinc* centum patrimonia causidicorum.   c) *Of cause or source,* c) *above.* 1¹¹⁹ quid facient comites quibus *hinc* toga, calceus *hinc* est?, i. e. from the *sportula.*   1¹⁴⁴ *hinc* subitae mortes.   6⁴⁶³, 10²⁷⁶, 12¹²⁷,

---

¹ The Vulgate reading Tac. Agr. 28 is no longer accepted.   In both the passages from Pliny the MSS vary.

² For *hic, ibi, inde=tum* in Catullus see Overholthaus, *Syntaxis Catullianae Capita Duo,* p. 15.

14^{52}. This use of *hinc* occurs first in Ter. And. 99; then in Cicero, Vergil, Livy, and (more frequently) post-classical authors. Dr. II 185. d) *From this time, after that.*[1] 6^{295} nullum crimen abest . . . ex quo paupertas Romana perit, *hinc* fluxit ad istos et Sybaris colles. This usage is found in Vergil, and in post-Augustan prose and poetry. Hand III, p. 91, where see examples. e) *hinc atque inde, inde . . . atque hinc, inde . . . hinc,* etc. 1^{65} *hinc* atque inde patens, i. e. on both sides. 8^{195} finge tamen gladios inde atque *hinc* pulpita poni, i. e. balance death against the stage. 10^{44} *illinc . . . hinc.* 14^{13} inde . . . *hinc*, from this quarter . . . from that. 15^{51} inde . . . *hinc*, on one side . . . on the other. *Hinc* occurs in no similar combination in H. The usage belongs to all periods. Hand III, p. 87 fol. f) *In anaphora.* 6^{295}, 11^{127}. One of the characteristics of J.'s declamatory style is his frequent use of anaphora.[2] In this figure he uses also these adverbs: *hic* 1^{110}, *iam* 3^{188}, 4^{56}, *inde* 8^{105}, *nondum* 6^{15}, *qua* 7^{223}, *quando,* 1^{87}, *quo* 8^{142}, *sic* 6^{229}, *tanquam* 4^{117}, *tantum* 7^{31}, *tunc* 3^{214}, *unde* 2^{27}. Weise, *Vindiciae Juvenalianae*, p. 46.

huc, H. 9, J. 3. H. uses *huc* in the Ep. only A. P. 462.

In *J.:* 3^{206} sic inde *huc* omnes tanquam ad vivaria currunt; *huc* here=to Rome.

ibi, H. o, J. 7. H. uses *ibi* only Od. 2. 6^{22}.

In *J.:* a) =*among them at that time.* 6^{324} O quantus tunc illis mentibus ardor concubitus; . . . nil *ibi* per ludum simulabitur. b) =*in that case.* 8^{64} sed venale pecus Coryphaei posteritas . . . si rara iuga victoria sedit : nil *ibi* maiorum respectus. 11^{176}.

I find no reason for H.'s avoiding *ibi*: nor can I discover any substitute for it.

ibidem, H. o, J. 1. 5^{40} tibi non committitur aurum, vel si quando datur, custos adfixus *ibidem*, i. e. at once, immediately. *Ibidem* in this sense is found Fin. 1. 6. 19 and elsewhere in Cicero, and the word is classical in both prose and poetry.

illic, H. 4, J. 17. In *H.: With no definite antecedent.* S. 1. 9^{48} non isto vivimus, *illic* . . . modo, i. e. at the house of Macaenas.

J.'s use of adverbs of place derived from personal pronouns is widely different from that of H. This difference may be sum-

---

[1] Servius ad A. 1^{194} *hinc* pro inde vel post.

[2] See the numerous examples cited by Weise, *Vindiciae Juvenalianae*, p. 45 ff. .

marily stated to be that J. departs further from the original local meaning of these words. It is well illustrated in the two authors' use of *illic.*

In *J.:* a) =*among them then.* 1^{91} posita sed luditur area. proelia quanta *illic* . . . videbis. Cf. *ibi* a) above. b) =*in that case.* 15^{91} sed res diversa, sed *illic* fortunae invidia est. Cf. *ibi* b) above. c) *With no definite antecedent.* 3^{98} nec tamen Antiochus nec erit mirabilis *illic* aut Stratocles, i. e. in Greece—to be inferred from the mention of Greek actors. 2^{159}, 3^{170}, 6^{410}, 13^{171}, 15^{12}. d) *Not essential to the meaning, but adding dramatic force.* 5^{71} finge tamen te inprobulum; superest *illic* qui ponere cogat. 6^{36} pusio . . . exigit a te nulla iacens *illic* munuscula. Here too, as in c) above, there is no definite antecedent. e) *illic . . . hic . . . illic.* 15^{7}. f) *In that, in it.* 10^{323} sive est haec Oppia sive Catulla deterior, talos habet *illic* femina mores.

illinc, H. 1, J. 4. In *J.:* 10^{11} *illinc* . . . *hinc.* See under *hinc* in J. e).

illuc, H. 5, J. 3. In *H.:* a) =*to that point—in the narrative.* S. 1. 1^{108} *illuc* unde abii redeo. 2^{23} si quis nunc quaerat quo res haec pertinet, *illuc*:[1] dum vitant . . . With this sentence of H. cf. J. 15^{72} a deverticulo, repetatur fabula. b) *To the following, to this.* S. 1. 3^{34} *illuc* praevertamur amatorem quod amicae turpia decipiunt.

H. uses *huc* literally 8 out of 9 times of its occurrence; *illuc* twice out of 5 times.

In *J.:* 12^{53} tunc adversis urgentibus *illuc* reccidit ut malum ferro submitteret.

inde, H. 8, J. 40. In *H.:* a) *From this cause.* S. 1. 1^{117} *inde* fit ut . . . Cf. eo fit . . . ut S. 1. 1^{56}, quo fit S. 2. 1^{32}. Lagergren, *De Vita et Elocutione Plinii,* p. 169, doubts whether *inde* causal occurs before the silver period. It is manifestly causal in the above passage from H., as also Cic. Mur. 12. 26, Livy 1. 32. 2, 25. 15. 16.[2] b) *From that time, after that.*[3] S. 1. 8^{3} olim truncus eram . . . deus *inde* ego. *Inde* in this sense occurs Ter. Heaut. 1. 1^{2}, Cic. Arch. 1. 1, and in Livy and post-Augustan writers. For examples consult Hand III, p. 366. Cf. *inde ab* Plaut. Trin. 2.

---

[1] For examples of *illuc* in this sense consult Hand III, pp. 217-18. The usage belongs to all periods.

[2] Cf. Hand III, pp. 364 and 370. Hand seems wrong in citing Ov. M. 2^{132}. See also Krebs II, p. 659.

[3] So Kiessling on S. 1. 8^{3}.

2^{21}, Capt. 3. 4^{112}, Ter. Heaut. 1. 2. 9, Cic. N. D. 2. 48. 124.   c) *For tum, postea.* S. 2. 6^{98} haec ubi dicta agrestem pepulere, domo levis exsilit; *inde* ambo propositum peragunt iter. For this usage see under *inde* in J. b). d) *From it, out of it.* S. 1. 8^{26} cruor in fossam confusus ut *inde* manis elicerent.

In *J.*: a) *From this cause,* a) *above.* 1^{168} *inde* irae et lachrimae. 3^{113} scire volunt secreta domus atque *inde*[1] timeri. Parataxis with *inde* here expresses what H. would have expressed with *ut* and the subjunctive—hypotaxis.[1] Juvenal sometimes uses parataxis with marked rhetorical effect, e. g. 3^{100}, 8^{25}, 13^{227}, $6^{:::}$. The above use of *inde*, occurring very rarely in classical times (see under *inde* a) in H.), and not found in Curtius, occurs 30 times in Pliny the Younger and 22 times in Tacitus.[2]   b) =*tum, postea.* 6^{312} inque vices equitant ac luna teste moventur; *inde* domos redeunt. For examples of *inde* in this sense in classical and post-classical prose and poetry consult Hand III, pp. 368–9. Cf. Kühnast, *Livianische Syntax,* p. 348. Ἔνθεν is similarly used in Greek. c) *From it, from him, or from them.* Cf. d) in H. 6^{62} cuneis an habent spectacula totis quod securus ames quodque *inde* excerpere possis. 6^{612}, 9^{28}, 10^{140}. d) 9^{20} deprehendas animi tormenta et gaudia; sumit utrumque *inde* habitum facies. e) *inde . . . si.* 6^{560} *inde* fides artis . . . si longo castrorum in carcere mansit. f) *inde . . . quod.* 15^{36} *inde* furor vulgo quod numina vicinorum odit uterque locus. g) *inde atque hinc, hinc atque inde, hinc . . . inde, inde . . . atque alia parte.* See under *hinc* e). Weise, *Vindiciae Juvenalianae,* p. 53, mentions the following cases of ellipsis, "*concitato dicendi generi maxime consentanea,*" where clauses are introduced by *hinc, inde,* and *unde* in J.: 1^{144} *hinc* subitae mortes. 15^{51}. 1^{168} *inde* irae et lacrimae. 3^{236}, 6^{560}, 7^{103}, 9^{27}, $15^{35,\ 45}$. 1^{150} *unde* ingenium par materiae? 2^{127}, 6^{286}, 9^{x}, 15^{108}.

Instead of *inde* causal H. uses: a) *eo.* For examples see under *eo* c), and with *eo quod* cf. *inde . . . quod* f) above. b) *hoc.* S. 1. 1^{46} non tuus *hoc* capiet venter plus ac meus. 3^{93}, $6^{41,\ 52,\ 110}$, 9^8, 10'. J. does not use *hoc.* H. does not use *hoc* in the Ep., and *eo* only A. P. 222, employing *ideo* and *idcirco* instead.[3] *Eo* and *hoc* are allowed in the S. of H. because of the prose character of

---

[1] Parataxis occurs, however, to some extent in H., more especially in the Satires, where its use is due mainly to the element of the *sermo familiaris.*

[2] Vogel on Curt. 9. 1. 33, Reisig N. 435.

[3] Of these two words only *idcirco* occurs in the S.—1. 4^{45}.

those compositions.[1]   To express causal relation H. uses also *ob hanc rem* S. 1. 3[81], 4[23]. *ob id factum* Ep. 2. 2[32]. *ob hoc* A. P. 393.

interius, H. 0, J. 1.   11[15] *interius* si attendas.   Cf. Cic. De Or. 3. 49. 190 ne insistat *interius*.

introrsum, H. 2, J. 0.   S. 2. 1[65] *introrsum* turpis.   Ep. 1. 16[43] *introrsum* turpem.

In the sense of *intus*, *introrsum* occurs already Caes. B. G. 7. 27.   For other examples see Hand III, p. 444.

intus, H. 7, J. 1.   In *H.:* S. 2. 3[115] si positis *intus* Chii . . . mille cadis.   So 3[112], A. P. 389.

From two examples of his use of *intus* H.'s fondness for philosophical reflection[2] comes out: S. 2. 1[32] cornu taurus petit ; unde nisi *intus* monstratum ? A. P. 108.

istic, H. 1, J. 1.   In *H.:* Ep. 1. 14[37] non *istic* obliquo oculo mea commoda quisquam limat.   *Istic* here="There where you are."

In *J.:* 3[29] cedamus patria: vivant Artorius *istic* et Catullus. *Istic* here has a contemptuous force.

istinc, H. 2, J. 1.[3]   In *H.:* S. 1. 4[131] quis ignoscas vitiis teneor : fortassis et *istinc* largiter abstulerit longa aetas.   Other examples of *istinc* for *ex* + the ablative are Plaut. Ps. 4. 7[6], Rud. 4. 4[13], Cat. 76[11].   Cf. *inde* d) in H. and *hinc* b) in H.   Ep. 1. 7[32] si vis . . . effugere *istinc*.

In *J.:* 8[105] inde Dolabella atque *istinc* Antonius, inde Verres referebant . . . spolia.   Cf. *hinc* e) in J.

The only examples of *istic* or *istinc* I find in post-Augustan Latin, other than the examples from Juvenal, are Luc. 7[592] (*istic*) and Mart. 1. 19[4] (*istinc*).   J.'s use of them is a mark of his forcible style.

nusquam, H. 4, J. 2.   In *H.:* a) S. 2. 5[102] ergo nunc Dama sodalis *nusquam* est ?, i. e. is he gone ?   For this usage consult Hand IV, p. 349, and cf. Cic. Tusc. 1. 6. 11.   b) *With a verb implying motion.* S. 2. 7[29] *nusquam* es . . . vocatus ad cenam. *Usquam* is so used S. 1. 1[37], 2. 1[31], 7[30].   This usage belongs mainly

---

[1] Cf. Beste, *De generis dicendi inter Horatii Carmina Sermonesque discrimine*, p. 45.

[2] On the relation of H. to philosophy consult the work of Kirchoff, Hildesheim, 1873.

[3] Here I follow the reading of the Pithoeanus and Buecheler against the other MSS and editors.   The archaic adverb, though very rare in post-Augustan Latin, is supported by *istic* 3[29].

to the conversational style, and naturally occurs oftenest in the Comedians and Cicero's Letters.[1]

obiter, H. o, J. 2. a) 3[211] *obiter* leget aut scribet—i. e. on the way. b) 6[481] verberat atque *obiter* faciem linit—i. e. incidentally, *en passant.*

Obiter appears to have come into literature from the language of the people. The only author to use it before Petronius is Laberius the mimographer. Pliny the Elder employs it frequently, and it occurs in Seneca, Quintilian, and Appuleius.[2]

passim, H. 2, J. o. Ep. 2. 1[117] scribimus indocti doctique poemata *passim*—i. e. *promiscue*, indiscriminately. *Passim* in this sense is rare: Tib. 2. 3[72], Just. 43. 1. 4.

peregre, H. 2, J. o. S. 1. 6[102] rusve *perigreve* exirem. Ep. 1. 12[13].

Peregre is a prose word. It occurs nowhere in poetry except in the Comedians and H.

porro, H. 4, J. 4. · In *H.:* a) *Literally "farther."* Ep. 1. 13[18] nitere *porro*. This usage is not common. It is found oftenest in ante-classical Latin. Livy 1. 7. 6 *porro* agere, 9. 2. 8 *porro* ire. b) *Furthermore, next.* S. 1. 3[101], Ep. 1. 6[34]. c) *Furthermore, moreover.* Ep. 1. 16[65] qui cupiet metuet . . .: *porro* que metuens vivit liber . . . non erit.

In *J.:* In all four cases *porro=furthermore, moreover*, c) above. 3[126], 6[240] utile *porro* filiolam . . . producere turpem.

post, H. 8, J. 1. In *H.:* a) S. 1. 6[61] nono *post* mense. b) *primum . . . post, prius . . . post.* A. P. 76 querimonia primum, *post* etiam inclusa est . . . sententia. A. P. 111 format . . . nos natura prius ad omnem fortunarum habitum: . . . *post* effert animi motus . . .

In *J.:* Of *place, behind* or *from behind.* 6[301] Andromachen a fronte videbis, *post* minor est. H. does not use *post* thus.

Instead of *post* b) in H., J. uses *deinde*—which occurs only three times in H., *tunc*, or *inde*. (See under *deinde*.) I find in J. no equivalent expression for *post paulo*, occurring three times in H. (J. uses *paulo ante* 6[227], 9[114].)

procul, H. 7, J. 6. In *H.:* *Joined with the ablative without a preposition.* S. 1. 6[52] prava ambitione *procul*. For this usage see under *simul* d) below.

---

[1] Cf. Schmalz, *Ueber den Sprachgebrauch des Asinius Pollio*, p. 42.
[2] Consult further Hand IV, p. 362 ff., and Krebs II, p. 169.

In *J.:* 14⁴⁵ *procul*, a *procul* inde. Weidner quotes Ov. M. 15⁵⁸⁰ procul, O procul este profani.[1] So ἑκάς in Greek; ἑκὰς ἑκὰς ὅστις ἀλιτρός (Kallim. in Apoll. 2).

prope, H. 16, J. 1. H uses *prope=almost* 10 times. For "almost" J. uses *fere* 6²¹², 11¹¹², *paene* 3 times. H. uses *fere* thus only S. 1. 3⁹⁶, *paene* 6 times. For "near" H. uses *prope* 6 times. J. uses thus *prope* 9¹⁰⁶, *iuxta* 11¹⁶⁵. With stantem *prope* H. S. 2. 5¹² and *propius* stes A. P. 361 cf. J. 3¹¹ substitit *ad* . . . arcus.

qua, H. 4, J. 1. H. uses *qua* in anaphora S. 1. 2⁵⁰ *qua* res, *qua* ratio suaderet. Other adverbs used in this figure by H. are: *aeque* Ep. 1. 1²³, *clare* Ep. 1. 16⁵⁹, *saepe* S. 1. 3¹¹·¹², Ep. 1. 17⁵⁵·⁵⁶, 19¹⁹·²⁰, *sic* Ep. 2. 1¹⁷⁹.

J uses *qua* in anaphora 7²²³. For a list of other adverbs used by J. in this figure see under *hinc* f) in J.

quatenus, H. 3, J. 1. H. uses *quatenus* only in its causal sense: S. 1. 1⁶⁴ iubeas miserum esse, libenter *quatenus* id facit. 3⁷⁶, 2. 4⁵⁷. So also J. 12¹⁰². *Quatenus* causal appears first Lucr. 2⁹²⁷. Then it does not occur till H. and Ov. M. 8⁷⁸⁶, 14⁴⁰, T. 5. 5²¹. The first example from prose appears to be Val. Max. 9. 11, and it is found, though still rarely, in Quintilian, Tacitus, Pliny, Suetonius, and later.[2]

quo, H. 30, J. 6. In *H.:* a) *Wherefore, for which reason.* S. 2. 1¹² *quo* fit ut. b) *To what purpose?, for what?* S. 1. 1⁷³ nescis *quo* valeat nummus? 6²⁴, Ep. 1. 5¹².

In *J.:* J. uses *quo=to what purpose?, for what?* 4 times. 8⁹ effigies *quo* tot bellatorum, si luditur alea pernox? 8¹⁴²·⁴, 14¹³⁵, 15⁶¹.

Anaphora occurs 8¹⁴²·⁴.

H. uses *quo=whither* 25 times, J. twice.

quorsum, H. 5, J. 0. *To what purpose?, for what?* S. 2. 3²⁰¹, 7¹¹⁶ *quorsum* est opus? Cf. Cic. Red. ad Quir. 2. 5, Leg. 1. 1. 4, Brut. 85. 292.[3]

superne, H. 2, J. 0. S. 2. 7⁶⁴, A. P. 4 mulier formosa *superne*.

ubi (loci), H. 11, J. 16. In *H.:* a) *=in quo, in quibus.* S. 1. 3⁶⁰ cum genus hoc inter versemur *ubi.* . . . 2. 3⁴⁸, 6² hortus *ubi.* 6¹⁰², Ep. 1. 6⁴⁵. This usage belongs in its origin to the style of conversation, just as the English "where" for "in which." b) *ubi* . . . *hic.* S. 2. 3²²⁰ *ubi* prava stultitia, hic summa est insania.

[1] Cf. also the note of Mayor.
[2] Wölfflin, Archiv V, pp. 405 ff., Dr. II 680.
[3] For this usage consult Krebs II, p. 427.

In *J.*: a) *In a case in which.* 3²⁸⁹ si rixa est *ubi* tu pulsas, ego vapulo tantum. b) *Postpositive.* 3²⁵ fatigatas *ubi* Daedalus exuit alas. 6¹⁵⁹, 10¹⁹⁴, 12⁸⁷, 15⁵. Weise thinks that among poets J. is especially fond of the postpositive for relative and interrogative words and for conjunctions.[1]

ubicumque, H. 2, J. 1. H. S. 1. 2⁶² rem oblimare malum est *ubicumque.* I find no example of *ubicumque* indefinite before this. After H. it is found Ov. Am. 3. 10⁵, Quint. 7. 4. 18, 10. 7. 28.

unde (inter.), H. 13, J. 14. In *H.:* a) *From what source ?—in the transferred sense.* S. 1. 5² cornu taurus petit ; *unde* nisi intus monstratum? 2. 2¹⁸. 2. 2³¹ *unde* datum sentis lupus hic Tiberinus an alto captus hiet? 2. 3¹⁷ sed *unde* tam bene me nosti? 2. 5²⁰. Ep. 2. 1¹¹³. b) *unde domo.* Ep. 1. 7⁵³ abi, quaere et refer *unde* domo, quis . . . Cf. Verg. A. 7¹¹⁴ *unde* domo, and the same expression Sen. Cons. Helv. 6. 3. Orelli states that *unde domo* frequently occurs in inscriptions, and compares the Greek πόθεν οἰκόθεν (Wilkins on Ep. 1. 7⁵³). c) *unde unde.* S. 1. 3⁸⁸. See under *Doubling of Adverbs.*

In *J.:* a) *From what source ?—in the transferred sense, as* a) above. 2¹²⁷ *unde* nefas tantum Latiis pastoribus? 7¹⁸⁸ *unde* igitur tot Quintilianus habet saltus? 9⁸, 10³², 14⁵⁶, 15¹⁰⁸. b) *In anaphora.* 2²⁷.

unde (rel.), H. 13, J. 16. In *H.:* a) *From which fact, from which source, from which cause.* S. 1. 2⁵⁸, 2⁷⁸, 2. 3²⁵, A. P. 252. (Cf. Krebs, II, p. 629.) b) *Of persons, "from whom."* S. 2. 3³³ Stertinius . . . *unde* ego . . . descripsi . . . praecepta haec. 6²¹. c) Ep. 2. 2⁴⁹ civilis . . . belli me tulit aestus in arma . . . : *unde* simul primum me dimissere Philippi. *Unde* here=*ab armis.*

In *J.:* a) *Causal.* 4⁹⁸ *unde* fit ut. Cf. *inde* fit ut H. S. 1. 1¹¹⁷. b) *Postpositive.* 6¹³⁹ illuc, testiculi sibi conscius *unde* fugit mus. See under *ubi* b) above. c) 7⁷⁶ nec defuit illi *unde* emeret multa.

usquam, H. 5, J. 3. See under *nusquam* b).

utrobique, H. 1, J. 0. Ep. 1. 6¹⁰ qui timet his adversa fere miratur eodem quo cupiens pacto: pavor est *utrobique* molestus. I find no other example of this word in poetry, except Plaut. Cist. 4. 2²¹.

2. *Adverbs of Time.*

adhuc,[2] H. 6, J. 13. In *H.:* a) *"Still," "yet"—with a verb in the present tense.* Ep. 1. 12¹⁵ *adhuc* sublimia cures. 2. 2¹¹⁴, A.

---

[1] See examples Weise, *Vindiciae Juvenalianae,* p. 57 ff.

[2] For the various uses of *adhuc* consult Hand I, pp. 156–157, Schmalz in Müller's *Handbuch der klassi. Alterthumswissenschaft* II, p. 554, Riemann, *Etudes sur Tite-Live,* p. 237.

P. 78. b) *"Still," "yet"—with a present participle.* A. P. 115
adhuc florente inventa. *Adhuc* with a participle or adjective is
not common until Livy and post-Augustan Latin. c) *"Still,"*
"yet"—with the gerundive. Ep. 1. 17³ *adhuc* docendus.

In *J.*: a) *As* a) *above.* 3²¹⁵ ardet *adhuc.* 6¹⁹³, ⁵⁰², 15³⁵. b) *"Still,"*
"yet"—with an adjective. 3¹¹¹ levis *adhuc.* 4¹⁰, 6¹²⁹, ²²⁸, 7¹⁹⁶,
10¹¹⁶, 13⁴¹. Cf. the remark under b) above. c) *With the gerun-*
dive, as c) above. 12¹⁵ *adhuc* horrenda. d) *"Still," "yet"—with*
*a comparative.*¹ 8³⁶ nomen erit pardus tigris leo, seu quid *adhuc*
est quod fremat in terris violentius. This usage belongs to silver
Latin.²

alias, H. 3, J. o. *Alias* means "at another time" in H. S. 1.
4⁶³, 9⁷², Ep. 2. 1¹⁷.

aliquando, H. o, J. 3. In all three examples from J. *aliquando*
has the meaning *nonnunquam, interdum.* In this sense it occurs
in Cicero and is common in post-classical Latinity.

ante, H. 2, J. 9. In *H.*: S. 2. 3¹⁵⁶ non *ante* . . . dementam
actum . . . quam . . . ferrum tepefecit. J. does not thus sepa-
rate *ante* and *quam.*

In *J.*: a) *Limited by paulo.* 6²²⁷ ornatas paulo *ante* fores. 9¹¹¹.
b) *ante* . . . *deinde.* 6⁴¹⁷ dominum iubet *ante* feriri, deinde
canem. This use of *ante* for *primum* is post-Augustan.³ c) *With*
an adjective. 3¹¹¹ filius *ante* pudicus. This usage is rare. In
Tacitus it occurs only An. 14. 7. 8 *ante* ignaros. Instead of
adverbial *ante* H. uses *prius,* which occurs in H. 10 times, in J. 3
times. Of course neither author uses *antĕā.*

brevi, H. 1, J. o. Ep. 1. 3⁹ *brevi* venturus in ora.

breviter, H. o, J. 1. 12¹²⁵ omnia soli . . . Pacuvio *breviter*
dabit.

dehinc, H. 2, J. o. a) =*tum, postea.* S. 1. 3¹⁰⁴ donec verba
. . . invenere; *dehinc* absistere bello coeperunt. This usage is
poetical and post-Augustan: Verg. A. 1¹³¹, ²⁵⁶, 5⁷²², 6⁶⁷⁸, Ov. F. 6⁷⁸⁷.
For post-Augustan examples see Hand II, p. 230. b) =*deinde.*
A. P. 144 non fumum exfulgore, sed ex fumo dare lucem cogitat,
ut speciosa *dehinc* miracula promat. *Dehinc* is thus used Epod.
16⁶⁵. *Dehinc* in this sense is not common. The only pre-
Augustan example appears to be Sall. Cat. 32 primum . . .

---

¹ Here Weidner takes *adhuc* as=*insuper,* πρὸς τούτοις. The climax and the
sense favor joining it with *violentius.*

² Krebs I, p. 87; Riemann, *Etudes sur Tite-Live,* p. 239.

³ For examples from Pliny and Celsus see Hand I, p. 376.

dehinc. Then Verg. G. 3[167], Sen. Quaest. Nat. 3[296], Sil. 8[473], Suet. Aug. 49.

dein, H. 2, J. 1. H. S. 1. 3[101], 5[97], J. 15[53]. Both poets use *dein* as a monosyllable. *Deinceps* H. uses as a dissyllable S. 28[80].

deinceps, H. 1, J. o. S. 2. 8[50]. I find no other example of *deinceps* in poetry until Prudentius.

deinde, H. 3, J. 12. Where *deinde* might have been employed H. uses: a) *tum* S. 1. 5[54], 7[28], 2. 3[50], 8[36, 78, 90]. b) *tunc* S. 2. 2[121], A. P. 103. J. also uses *tunc* thus 6[607], 10[287], 12[53], 13[107]. c) *postmodo* S. 2. 6[27]. d) *dehinc* A. P. 144. e) *inde* S. 2. 6[9]. J. also so uses *inde* 6[312], 11[47]. f) *post* S. 1. 4[68], A. P. 76 primum ... *post,* A. P. 111. g) *post hunc, post hanc, post hoc, post haec, post hos.* S. 1. 6[122], 2. 2[123], 8[31], Ep. 1. 8[13], 2. 1[175], 2[28], A. P. 278, 401. J. also uses *post hunc,* etc., thus: 1[33], 2[62], 5[116], 6[499]. h) *subinde* Ep. 1. 8[15] primum ... *subinde.* i) *denique* Ep. 1. 7[6], 2. 2[5].

demum, H. 1, J. o. S. 1. 5[23]. The post-Augustan poets appear to have avoided *demum.*[1] H. does not use it in the Odes, but Vergil uses it freely, and it occurs in Ovid.

denique, H. 15, J. o. a) *At all events, in any case.* S. 1. 2[133] ne nummi pereant aut puga aut *denique* fama. Ep. 2. 2[127].[2] b) = *deinde.* Ep. 1. 7[68] ille Philippo quod non mane domum venisset, *denique* quod non providisset eum. c) *In the end, at last.* A. P. 267 an omnis visuros peccata putem mea tutus et intra spem veniae cautus? vitavi *denique* culpam, non laudem merui.

Where *denique* might have been used, J. sometimes employs *tandem,* which occurs 11 times, in H. 7 times. *Denique* is found in Martial.

dudum, H. o, J. 2. *For iam dudum.* 3[129] cum praetor lictorem impellat et ire praecipitem iubeat, *dudum* vigilantibus orbis. 10[333] *dudum* sedet illa parato flammeolo. This usage is very rare.[3] The only examples I find, other than the above, are Cic. Att. 4. 5 and Pliny, H. N. 19. 1. 2.[4]

hodie, H. 9, J. 6. In *H.:* a) *At the present day.* S. 2. 2[46], Ep. 2. 1[160]. b) *Expressing impatience.* S. 2. 7[21] non dices *hodie* quorsum haec tam putida tendant, furcifer? Ep. 1. 7[19] ut libet:

---

[1] The only example I find is Pers. 1[61].
[2] For other examples of this usage see Hand, II 270.
[3] *iam dudum* is now read Ter. Heaut. 4. 5[10].
[4] Here the MSS are divided between *nam dudum* and *non dudum.* The reading is so near *iam* dudum that some have preferred to read so. Sillig reads *nam dudum.*

haec porcis *hodie* comedenda relinques.[1] Cf. Ter. Eun. 4. 4[45]
possumne ego *hodie* ex te exsculpere verum? Phor. 5. 3[72]. This
usage belongs to the style of conversation. c) *hodie, cras.* Ep.
1. 16[33] qui dedit hoc *hodie*, cras auferet.

In *J.*: a) *As* a) *above.* 13[17]. b) *hodie . . . here . . . cras.* 3[27]
res *hodie* minor est here quam fuit, atque eadem cras deteret
exiguis aliquid.

iam, H. 33, J. 97. In *H.*: a) *At last, at length.* S. 1. 1[5] miles
ait multo *iam* fractus membra labore. 5[20], 2. 6[100], Ep. 1. 1[2], 7[11], 7[47],
10[11], 18[32], 2. 1[148], A. P. 468. Ἤδη is similarly used in Greek. b)
At once, forthwith, presently. S. 1. 1[16] si quis deus 'en ego,' dicat,
'*iam* faciam quod voltis.' 8[33], 2. 3[151], 4[29], 7[74]. c) *In a transition—
for iam vero.* Ep. 2. 1[6]. *iam* Saliare Numae carmen qui laudat.[2]
d) *iam . . . cum.* S. 1. 5[20] *iam*que dies aderat nil cum procedere
lintrem sentimus. 2. 6[100]. e) *iam . . . iam*, for *modo . . . modo.*
5. 2. 7[13] *iam* moechus Romae, *iam* mallet doctus Athenis vivere.
2. 7[20], 7[114]. This usage is rare even in poetry. In prose: Livy,
30. 30. 10,[3] Vell. 2. 114. 2, Pliny, Ep. 7. 27. 8, Flor. 2. 17. 8, 3. 1.
10.[4] f) *iam nunc.* Ep. 2. 1[127] *iam nunc . . .* mox. A. P. 43 ut
iam nunc dicat *iam* nunc debentia dici. Cf. Odes 2. 1[17]. g) *iam
simul.* Ep. 2. 2[205] quid? cetera *iam* simul isto cum vitio fugere?

In *J.*: a) *At last, at length*, a) *above.* This use of *iam* occurs
in J. 40 times: 2[10], 3[206], 4[56, 57, 135, 138, 303], 5[17, 166, 168], 6[105, 127, 153, 215, 302, 325,
329, 360, 370, 377, 442, 485, 574], 7[170, 210], 8[97, 155], 9[49, 79, 86], 10[195, 199. 270], 11[127, 157], 13[14,
218], 15[62, 91], 16[56]. a') *By this time, at length.* 4[303], 5[48, 93], 10[204], 12[30,
69], 13[9] casus multis hic cognitus ac *iam* tritus. b) *At once, forthwith, presently*, b) *above.* 1[130] nullus *iam* parasitus erit. 4[135], 12[86].
c) *iam . . . iam*, e) *above.* 16[46]. d) *iam nunc*, f) *above.* 11[204],
14[230]. e) *iam iam.* 6[62n]. See under *Doubling of Adverbs* below.
f) *At the present day.* 4[101], 6[749], 11[50], 14[276], 15[112, 150] mundi principio
indulsit . . . conditor . . .: sed *iam* serpentum maior concordia.
As to *iam* used thus for *nunc* see Hand, III, p. 125 fol. g) *Of
the present as opposed to the past.* 4[32] *iam* princeps equitum . . .
qui . . . solebat vendere . . . siluros. 6[43]. h) *Truly, indeed.* 10[28]
*iam*ne igitur laudas quod de sapientibus alter ridebat . . .? 15[56,
117]. i) *In anaphora.* 3[168], 4[56].

The large difference between the number of times *iam* occurs

---

[1] Kiessling renders *noch heute.*
[2] Schütz renders *nun vollends.*
[3] Cf. Weissenborn's note.
[4] Cf. Wölfflin, Archiv, II, p. 245.

in H. and in J. is due to J.'s great fondness for the uses a) and a')
above. This is a mark of his vivid, excited style. So 4^{138} noverat
ille luxuriam imperii veterem noctesque Neronis *iam* medias.
6^{302}, 13^{14}, and elsewhere.

interea, H. 2, J. 14. The disproportion in the use of this word
by H. and J. may be accounted for by its use in J. with the force
of an adversative particle, while H. does not so employ it. Thus
1^{135} caulis miseris atque ignis emendus; optima silvarum *interea*
pelagique vorabit rex. 2^{137} *interea* tormentum ingens nubentibus
haeret; 5^{120}, $6^{237, \ 481, \ 508}$, 10^{342}, $11^{14, \ 193}$, 14^{138}. As to this usage,
occurring already in Cic., consult Hand, III, p. 416; Krebs, I, p.
703 fol.

modo, H. 18, J. 19. In *H.*: a) *modo ... interdum, modo ...
saepe, saepe ... modo*. S. 1. 9^9 ire *modo* ocius, interdum consistere. 2. 7^7, S. 1. 10^{11} *modo* tristi, saepe iocoso. 2. 7^9 saepe ...
modo. This sequence is found mainly in H., Ovid, and silver
prose-writers.[1] To the examples from classical prose-writers cited
by Wölfflin, Archiv, II 252 fol.,[2] add Nep. Att. 20. 2. b) *Only,
just—with an imperative*. S. 2. 3^{276} adde cruorem stultitiae atque
ignem gladio scrutare *modo*, inquam.[3]

In *J.*: a) *modo ... nunc ... nunc*. 14^{6}. Cf. the same sequence,
Ovid, T. 1. 2^{27}, and *modo ... nunc*, M. 13^{921}. b) 15^{119} quis *modo*
casus impulit hos? The explanation of Mayor and Weidner for
modo here seems unsatisfactory. The word serves to call the
attention in a transition, as the Greek δή, our 'now,' and *iam*
H. Ep. 2. 1^{96}. See under *iam* c) above. c) *Limiting a verbal
noun*. 2^{73} *modo* victor. Cf. signator *falso* 1^{67}, and *sic* i) in H.

olim, H. 23, J. 19. In *H.*: a) *At times, ofttimes*.[4] S. 1. 1^{25} ut
pueris *olim* dant crustula blandi doctores. Ep. 1. 10^{42}. This use
of *olim* is ante-classical and poetical. It occurs in Plautus, Lucil.
130 (Lach.), Vergil, H. Od. 4. 4^5, Epod. 3^1, and in Ovid. b)
Hereafter, some day. S. 1. 4^{137} numquid ego illi imprudens *olim*
faciam simile? 6^{83}, 2. 5^{27}, Ep. 1. 3^{14}, A. P. 386. H. uses *olim* of an
event which has occurred during his life-time, S. 1. $6^{47, \ 54}$. Cf.
also S. 1. 3^{73}, 2. 3^{70}.

In *J.*: a) *Sometimes, ofttimes*, a) *above*. 10^{142} patriam tamen

[1] For examples see Hand, III, pp. 647-48.

[2] In his paper *Was heist bald ... bald?*

[3] Fritzsche, Schütz and Palmer place a period after *scrutare* and throw
modo inquam with the next sentence. I prefer to read as above. So Orelli
and Kiessling.

[4] Servius ad A. 8^{391} atque *olim* fere ut solet.

obruit *olim* gloria paucorum. b) *Hereafter, some day,* b) *above.*
14^{225}. c) = *iamdudum.* 4^{96} sed *olim* prodigio par est cum nobili-
tate senectus. 6$^{42, 90}$ famam contempserat *olim.* I find no example
of *olim* in this sense before Seneca and Lucan.[1] Tacitus uses *olim*
thus 16 times. For examples from other writers see Mayor on J.
4^{06}, Lagergren *De Vita et Elocutione Plinii*, p. 170, and Hand
IV, pp. 370–371. Similarly πάλαι is used in Greek.[2]

protinus, H. 3, J. 7. In *H.*; S. 2. 5^{21} tu *protinus* unde divitias
. . . ruam die, augur. *Protinus* meaning *at once, immediately,*[3] is
not common in prose until Livy. Cic. Inv. 2. 15. 20, Caes. B. G.
2. 9, 5. 17, B. C. 1. 14.

In *J.*: In every example[4] in J., *protinus* means *straightway, at
once.* With 14^{123} sunt quaedam vitiorum elementa; his *protinus*
illos imbuit cf. H. Ep. 2. 1^{127} os tenerum pueri . . . poeta figurat,
torquet ab obscaenis *iam nunc* sermonibus. To express "at
once," "immediately," H. uses *continuo* S. 1. 2^{118}, 6$^{29, 100}$, 2. 3^{160}, 8^{29}.
J. also uses *continuo*, 6^{493}, 13^{191}, 14^{243}.

quando, H. 17, J. 23. H. uses *quando* interrogative but 3 times,
J. 14 times. H. does not use *quando = when* except as interroga-
tive,[5] J. only 12^{55}. J. uses *si quando* 3^{173}, 5^{40}, 8^{80}, 12^{23}. Instead of
si quando H. uses *quandocumque, quandoque,* or *quotiens.* See
under those words.

quandocumque, H. 3, J. 0. S. 1. 9^{33} garrulus hunc *quando*
consumet *cumque.* As regards this indefinite use of *quandocumque*
for *aliquando* cf. Ov. M. 6^{341}, 2. 3. 1^{57}, and the note of Schütz on
H. 5. 1. 9^{33}. Other examples of tmesis will be found under *Adverbs in -tenus.*

quandoque, H. 1, J. 3. In *H.*; A. P. 359 indignor *quandoque*
bonus dormitat Homerus. For this use of *quandoque,* occurring
already in Cic., see Krebs, II 405. Cf. also Mützell and Vogee on
Curt. 7. 10. 9, Roby's Latin Grammar 2290.

In *J.*: In J. *quandoque* means only *some day,* of the future.
2^{x2} foedius hoc aliquid *quandoque* audebis amictu. 5^{172}, 14^{31}. In this
sense the word is mainly post-Augustan, only two examples being
quoted before silver Latin—Cic. Fam. 6. 19. 2, Livy 21. 3. 6.

[1] Verg. G. 4^{421}, it is more natural to take *olim* as *ofttimes.* So Koch,
Conington, and Papillon.
[2] Soph. O. T. 896, Aj. 20; Ar. Vesp. 1060; Plato Meno 91 A.
[3] Kiessling on Od. 3. 3^{30} denies this meaning of *protinus* for H. and Old
Latin.
[4] 3^{140}, 4^{48}, 7^{165}, 11^{190}, 13^{176}, 14^{123}, 16^{27}.
[5] S. 2. 2^{42} is a possible exception, but see Kiessling's note.

quoad, H. 1, J. 0. S. 2. 3⁹¹. *Quoad* here is a monosyllable.[1]
The above is the only undisputed example of *quoad* in poetry
after Plautus and Terence, so far as I can discover.[2]

quondam, H. 7, J. 7. In *H.*: a) *From time to time, sometimes.*
S. 2. 2⁸² hic tamen ad melius poterit transcurrere *quondam*, sive
diem festum rediens advexerit annum, seu³ ... Ep. 1. 18⁷⁸ falli-
mur, et *quondam* non dignum tradimus. It is questionable
whether Cicero uses *quondam* thus. Div. 1. 43. 98 and Fam. 2.
16. 2 are quoted, but consult Wilkins' note on H. Ep. 1. 18⁷⁸.
The word is found in this sense, however, H. Od. 2. 10¹ˣ, Verg.
A. 2³⁰⁷, Ov. M. 9¹⁷⁰, 8¹⁹¹. So the Greeks occasionally used ποτέ.[4]
b) *Limiting a verbal noun.* Ep. 2. 2¹⁶⁷ emptor ... *quondam*.
Cf. A. P. 443 nullum *ultra* verbum. Ep. 2. 1²³ *sic* fautor veterum.
Od. 3. 17⁹ *late* tyrannus. For the attributive use of adverbs in
Latin consult Dr. I 131 fol.; Reisig, 150 and note; Overholthaus,
Syntaxis Catullianae capita duo, p. 15; Uri, *Quatenus apud
Sallustium sermonis Latini plebeii aut cotidiani vestigia appa-
reant*, p. 121; Riemann, *Etudes sur Tite-Live*, p. 245; Dr., *Syn-
tax und Stil des Tacitus*, p. 8; Kraut, *Ueber Syntax und Stil des
jüngeren Plinius*, p. 25.

quotiens, H. 3, J. 19. The large use of this word is character-
istic of J. He employs it instead of *ubi* or *quandocumque*. See
under those words.

raro, H. 4, J. 0. S. 1. 1¹¹⁷, 4¹⁸, 2. 2⁵ᵇ, 3¹. J., in common with
the Latin poets generally, uses the corresponding adjective instead
of *raro*.[5] I find no example of *raro* in post-Augustan poetry
except Mart. 1. 93⁶, 5. 39³, 14. 213¹. Among the classical poets,
Lucr. 6¹⁴ˣ, ¹¹⁸⁶, Hor. Od. 3. 2¹¹, Verg. Cat. 7¹⁴, Ov. M. 13¹¹⁷. J. 8⁶³
si *rara* iugo victoria sedit, 5¹⁵, 10¹ˣ, 13ˣ.

repente, H. 0, J. 2. H. uses *subito* 4 times, J. only 3¹⁶⁹.

semel, H. 14, J. 5. In *H.*: a) *Once, once for all.* S. 1. 4³⁶ et
quodcumque *semel* chartis illeverit. 2. 1²⁴, 7⁷¹, Ep. 1. 2⁶⁸, 7⁹⁶, 10¹⁷,
17ⁱ⁵, 18⁷¹, A. P. 331, 452. b) *Once, only once.* Ep. 2. 2¹⁴ *semel* hic
cessavit. A. P. 468. c) *ut semel, si semel, cum semel.* S. 2. 1²⁴

---

[1] Brand, *Intersit. ne aliquid inter Horatii Flacci satiras et ejusdem epistolas*,
p. 38, puts down this monosyllabic use of *quoad* as an archaism.

[2] The usually accepted reading Lucret. 2⁸⁵⁰, 5¹²¹³, ¹⁴³³ is *quoad*, but Lachmann
reads *quo ad*.

[3] The Lexica take *quondam* here as = *some day* — of the future.

[4] Cf. Haupt on Ov. M. 9¹⁷⁰.

[5] Cf. Krebs II, p. 431.

saltat Milorius ut *semel* icto accessit fervo capiti. 2. 5^{81} si *semel*,
7^{71} cum *semel.* Ep. 1. 10^{17}, A. P. 331.

In *J.*: a) *Once, once for all,* a) *above.* 13^{242}. b) *Once, only
once,* b) *above.* 4^{143} et *semel* aspecti litus dicebat echini. c) *At
once, once for all.* 6^{321} ut quidquid subiti ... discriminis instat in
tunicas eat et totum *semel* expiet annum.

simul, H. 27, J. o.[1] a) *With me, in my company.* Ep. 1. 10^{50}
excepto quod non *simul* esses cetera laetus. Kiessling remarks
that this use of *simul* is colloquial, and compares Cic. Att. 6. 2. 8
scribis morderi te interdum quod non *simul* sis. b) *simul primum.* Ep. 2. 2^{19} unde *simul primum* me dimisere Philippi. This
combination is rare. Dr. II 601 pronounces it everywhere questionable. It is found Livy 6. 1. 6, 35. 44. 5. *Simul ac primum*
is used by Cicero Verr. 2. 13. 34, and by Suet. Jul. 30, Nero 43.
c) *In anaphora.* S. 2. 2^{73}. d) *As a preposition.* S. 1. 10^{86} simul
his. *Simul* with the ablative occurs first in H.; then Verg. A.
5^{337}, 11^{527}; Ov. T. 5. 10^{29}; Sen. Tro. 1045; Sil. 3^{268}, 5^{418}; Tac. An.
3. 64, 4. 55, 6. 9, 13. 34. *Procul* with the ablative occurs first in
H.; then Ov. Pont. 1. 5^{73}, 4. 9^{123}, and often in Livy and silver
writers.[2] e) *For simul atque.* S. 1.1^{36}, 2. 2$^{73, 74}$, 3^{226}, 6$^{32, 114}$, Ep. 1.
6^{11}, 7^{90}, 10^{8}, 19^{10}.

H.'s large use of *simul atque*—5 times, *simul ac*—5 times, and
simul = simul atque—10 times, is noteworthy. Instead of these
expressions, J. uses simply *cum* or *ut* with the indicative. So
1$^{142, 160}$, 3$^{122, 135}$, 4$^{60, 63}$, and elsewhere. Where *simul* might have
been written he uses *pariter* 6^{20} duae *pariter* sorores. 6$^{315, 328, 441, 576}$,
10^{309}, 13^{206}. Where *simul cum* might have been written he uses
simply *cum.* So 2^{158}, 3^{63}, 6$^{164, 171}$, and elsewhere. With H. S. 1.
10^{76} *simul* his (Pollio, Messala, and others) cf. J. 3^{99} *cum* molli
Demetrius Haemo. As J. uses *simul* not at all, so he employs
una but once, 15^{243}. Martial uses *una* only once (1. 96^{11}), and
simul only 10. 35^{17}, 11. 58^{10}.

tandem, H. 7, J. 11. In *H.*: Ep. 1. 17^{2} quamvis ... scis quo
tandem pacto deceat maioribus uti.[3] Wilkins states, in his note
on this passage, that no parallel has been adduced for this use of
tandem in a dependent question.

[1] The second hand of P, and almost all the minor MSS have *simul* 5^{142},
and so Mayor reads in his last edition. Buecheler and Weidner, however,
follow Jahn and read *semel.*

[2] Krebs II, p. 352 ff.

[3] Schütz thinks that *tandem* here has the force of *doch, nur,* and serves
merely to fix the attention.

23

tum, H. 15, J. 3. In *H.*: a) *Of future time.* S. 1. 2^{91}, 2. 5^{66} *tum* gener hoc faciet. b) *Then, thereupon.* See under *deinde* a). In *J.*: a) *tum cum* 7$^{10^s}$. b) *tunc . . . tum* in anaphora 6^{727}.

tunc, H. 3,^{1} J. 34. In *H.*: *Thereupon, then.* S. 2. 2^{121} bene erat . . . pullo atque haedo ; *tunc* pensilis uva secundas . . . ornabat mensas. A. P. 103. Cf. *deinde* b). This use of *tunc* is rare until after the Augustan period. Cic. Verr. 2. 2. 52, Fam. 3. 5. 3, 3. 6. 2, Livy 3. 70. 8, 7. 8. 1, 45. 25. 1. *Tunc* used thus is not found in Caesar or Vergil.

In *J.*: a) *As = thereupon, then.* 6^{607}, 10^{267}, 12^{53}, 13^{107}. See under *tunc* in H. b) *tunc . . . tum, in anaphora.* 6^{727}. c) *tunc cum*, *tunc . . . cum.* 13^{40}, 10^{328}. d) *tunc . . . quotiens.* 14^{21}. e) *Emphatic, "at that very time."* 2^{30} adulter . . . qui *tunc* leges revocabat amaras . . . ipsis Veneri Martique timendas.

ubi (temp.), H. 29, J. 1.^{2} In *H.*: *ubi + ablative absolute.* S. 2. 8^{10} *his ubi sublatis*, puer . . . mensam pertersit. In some cases in which H. would have used *ubi*, J. uses *quotiens*, which occurs in H. only 3 times, in J. 19 times.

ut (temp.), H. 10, J. 2.^{3}

3. *Adverbs of Manner and Degree.*

adeo, H. 4, J. 15. In all four examples from H.^{1} *adeo* is used normally—limiting an adjective. In no case is it accompanied by *usque* or any other particle. Nowhere does it follow its word.

In *J.*: a) *Limiting an adjective but following its word.* 5^{129} quis vestrum temerarius usque *adeo* . . . ut . . . 6^{50} paucae *adeo*. 6$^{1^{h2}}$ uis deditus autem usque *adeo* ut . . . 10^{297} rara est *adeo*. 13^{59}, 15^{h2}. This position of *adeo*, in the sense in which it is here used, is not common. Ter. Heaut. 5. 1^{12}, Verg. A. 1^{565}.^{5} b) *Introducing a clause—the conjunctive use.* 3^{274} *adeo* tot fata quot illa nocte patent vigiles . . . fenestrae. 11^{131} *adeo* nulla uncia nobis est eboris.

---

^{1} The MSS of H. favor *tunc*, S. 2. 2^{121}, 3^{304}, A. P. 103. So Keller and Holder read, and Keller states in his *Epilegomena zu Horaz*, note on S. 2. 3^{304}, that here the archetype undoubtedly had *tunc*. Schütz follows the MSS in all three cases. Palmer writes *tum* S. 2. 2^{121}, *tunc* 2. 3^{304}. Kiessling writes *tum* in all three cases, holding that H. does not use *tunc* before consonants. See his note on Epod. 17^{17}.

^{2} 11^{47}. ^{3} 4$^{60\ 63}$.

^{4} S. 1. 1^{13}, 7^1, Ep. 1. 1^{19}, 2. 1^{54}.

^{5} The former reading, Livy 4. 54. 4 *avidissimo adeo populo*, has been corrected to *avidissimo ad ea populo*.

13^{181} quantulacumque *adeo* est occasio sufficit irae.[1] This conjunc-tive use of *adeo*—where Cicero would have used *tantum*—is found first Verg. G. 2^{272}.[2] It is quite common in Livy, and occurs in Curtius, Quintilian, Tacitus, and later, in Lactantius. c) *With a verb.* 6^{59} *adeo* sennerunt Jupiter et Mars? 12^{16}, 14^{235}.

The large use of *adeo* in J. is to be accounted for by his fondness for ending a thought with a clause such as we introduce by *so, so great.* For this purpose he uses *adeo*, or some case of *tantus, -a, -um*. Examples of such a clause introduced by *adeo* are: 6^{50} auratam Iunoni caede iuvencam, si tibi contigerit capitis matrona pudici. paucae *adeo* Cereris vittas contingere dignae, quarum non timeat pater oscula. 10^{297}, 12^{16}, 13^{50}, 14^{235}, 15^{62}, and elsewhere. Examples of such a clause introduced by some case of *tantus, -a, -um* are: 6^{595} *tantum* artes huius ... possunt. 6^{626}, 7^{84}, 10$^{140, 238, 306}$, 13$^{58, 75}$, 14^{264}. The only cases of *tantus, -a, -um* so introducing a clause in H. are Ep. 2. 1^{203} *tanto* cum strepitu ludi spectantur, and A. P. 243 and 244.

alioqui, H. 2, J. 0. S. 1. 4^{1}, 6^{66}. This word appears to have been introduced into literature by H., and is used in poetry by him only.[3]

After H. *alioqui* is used by Livy, and is a favorite word in silver Latin.[4]

aliter, H. 1,[5] J. 4. In *J.*: a) *Otherwise, unless this be true.* 3^{281} ergo non *aliter* poterit dormire? b) *Differently, in the con-trary manner.* 6^{11} quippe *aliter* tunc orbe novo ... vivebant homines. c) *non aliter ... quam.* 6^{619}, 7^{220}.

Instead of *aliter* H. uses a) *haud ita* S. 2. 5^{1x}. b) *secus* A. P. 14^{9}. c) *alioqui*, for which see above.

bene, H. 43, J. 11. In *H.*: a) *With an adjective, = valde.*[6] S. 1. 3^{61} *bene* sano. 9^{14} *bene* sanae. H. so uses *male* S. 1. 3$^{31, 45}$, 4^{66},

---

[1] Here Mayor and Weidner take *adeo* as = *immo*. As this use of the word is not found elsewhere in J., and it seems quite natural to take it as = "to such an extent is it true that"—which use is found elsewhere in J.—I prefer so to take it.

[2] The passage Cic. Off. 1. 11. 37 is bracketed by the recent editors as a later interpolation. So Orelli and Baiter, Stickney, and C. F. W. Müller.

[3] Cf. Kiessling to S. 1. 4^{4}. The line Lucret. 3^{414} is rejected by Lachmann, while Monroe reads there *aliquoi*. Cf. also Reisig, N. 431 *b*.

[4] Cf. Ribbeck, Lat. Part., p. 20; Hand, I, p. 235 fol.

[5] Ep. 2. 2^{166}.

[6] Porphyrion to H. Od. 3. 24^{50} *bene* pro valde positum, ut apud Ennium frequenter.

9⁶⁵, 2. 5⁴⁹. For this usage in Latin consult Wölfflin, Archiv, I, p. 95 ff., and the references of Schmalz, *Ueber den Sprachgebrauch des Asinius Pollio*, p. 43. b) *bene est, bene erat.* S. 2. 2¹⁷⁰ *bene erat* ... *pullo atque haedo.* 6¹, 8¹, Ep. 1. 1⁸⁹, 12⁵ si ventri *bene*, si lateri est. Cf. Odes 3. 16⁴³ *bene* est. This usage belongs mainly to the style of conversation. c) S. 2. 21⁷¹ valeas *bene*. d) A. P. 428 clamabit enim 'pulchre, *bene*, recte.'

In *J.*: 10⁷² '*bene* habet: nil plus interrogo.' This same expression occurs Cic. Mur. 6. 14, Prop. 5 (4). 11⁹⁷, Livy 8. 6. 4, 9. 1, Stat. Th. 11⁵⁵⁷, 12³³⁸.[1] Cf. Mayor on J. 10⁷². In the conversational style of an author so fond of his ease as H. we should naturally expect a much larger use of a broad and for the most part colorless word like *bene* than in the vigorous and direct style of J. *Male* occurs 28 times in H., 4 times in J.

benigne, H. 3, J. o. a) *In declining an offer*, "I thank you." Ep. 1. 7¹⁶ 'at tu quantum vis tolle.' '*benigne*' ... 'ut libet.' 7⁶². This usage occurs in Plautus and Terence and Cic. Verr. 3. 85. 196. Schütz cfs. καλῶς in Greek.[2] b) *Freely, fully*. Ep. 1. 17¹¹ si prodesse tuis pauloque *benignius*. So Od. 1. 9⁶.

frustra, H. 8, J. o.[3] *Frustra* is used by almost every Latin poet, including Lucan, Statius, Silius and Martial. I find no substitute in J. He uses *nequiquam* 8²⁰⁵.

humane, H. 1, J. o. Ep. 2. 2⁷⁰ intervalla vides *humane* commoda. *Humane* is here used in irony, and has the force of *probe, admodum*. Cf. the notes of Schütz and Kiessling.

ita, H. 23, J. 4. In *H.*: a) *ita ut*. S. 1. 2³⁰ vix credere possis quam sibi non sit amicus, *ita* ut pater ille ... Cf. Caes. B. G. 1. 12 flumen est Ara ... incredibili lenitate, *ita* ut ..., and 1. 38. b) *In answering*, "Yes." S. 2. 7² 'Davus-ne?' '*ita*, Davus.' Cf. Ter. Eun. 4. 4⁵⁴, And. 5. 2⁸, Cic. Or. 2. 10. 43. c) *In adjuration*. S. 2. 2¹²¹ ac venerata Ceres, *ita* culmo surgeret alto, explicuit ... Similarly H. uses *sic* Od. 1. 3¹, S. 2. 3¹⁰⁰. d) *haud ita, non ita, followed by an adjective or adverb*. See under *haud* a) below. e) *atque ita porro*. S. 1. 3¹⁰¹ pugnis, dein fustibus, atque *ita* porro pugnabant armis.

In *J.*: a) *To mark a direct quotation*. 2⁷⁴ atque *ita* subridens, 'Felicia tempora ...' 13⁹¹. b) *With illative force*, "then," "so

---

[1] In all of these passages the expression is '*bene* habet' and in a direct quotation.

[2] Ar. Ran. 512.

[3] Cf. Wölfflin on *Frustra, nequiquam und Synonyma*, Archiv, II, p. 9 ff.

then." 6²²² 'pone crucem servo.' 'meruit quo crimine servus
...?' '... o demens, *ita* servus homo est?'

That H. uses *ita* so much oftener than J. is partially to be
accounted for by the fondness of the former for similes and com-
parisons. The colloquial element in H., too, has its influence
here; so b) and c) in H. above. H. uses *ita* twice for *tam*, which
usage is not found in J.

item, H. 2, J. o. S. 1. 3⁷⁷, A. P. 90. *Item* is not freely used in
poetry. Besides the examples just quoted from H., I find the
word only in Plautus and Terence, Cat. 61³⁶, Lucr. 5⁷³¹, Verg. G.
1¹⁸⁷, Culex 402. *Item* is doubtful for Tacitus, but occurs in Pliny
the Elder, Quintilian and Suetonius.

longe, H. 9, J. 8. In *H.*: a) *With the superlative.* S. 1. 5³
longe doctissimus. 5ⁿ, 6⁹². H. uses *multo* with a superlative
twice. S. 1. 5³⁹, 2. 3⁴². Only *multo* was used to strengthen the
superlative until Cicero, who used *longe* first Rosc. Am. 12. 33.
Then for a considerable time Cicero uses *longe* and *multo* almost
equally. In his latest writings *multo* is the exception. Caesar
uses only *longe*, Nepos only *multo*. Sallust uses *multo* 4 times,
longe once (Jug. 9. 2). Livy, Pliny the Elder, and Quintilian use
both *multo* and *longe* with the superlative. Only *multo* survives
in the Romance languages; showing that it was used rather than
longe in the language of daily life.[1] H. nowhere uses *longe* with
a comparative; notice, however, S. 2. 5⁷³ vincit *longe*. b) *longe
longeque*. S. 1. 6¹⁸. See under *Doubling of Adverbs.*

In *J.*: a) *Of time*. 7¹¹ *longe* ferrata domus. *Longe* temporal
occurs several times in Martial. b) *With a comparative.* 6²¹⁰
longe minus. This usage occurs Hirtius, B. A. 46. 4, B. H. 7. 5,
Sall. Hist. 3. 61. 9 D., Verg. A. 9⁵⁵⁶, Ov. M. 4²¹⁵, and in Livy, Velleius, Valerius Maximus, Curtius, Seneca, Quintilian, and other
silver writers.[2] I cannot parallel the example from J. of *longe*
with the comparative in any silver poet except Phaedrus. J. has
no example of a superlative limited by *longe, multo* or *multum*.

male, H. 28, J. 4. In *H.*: a) *With an adjective,* = *valde*. S.
1. 3⁷¹ *male* laxus. 3⁴⁵, 4⁶⁶, 9⁶⁵, 2. 5⁴⁵. For this usage see under
bene a), and Schmalz, *Ueber den Sprachgebrauch des Asinius*

---

[1] For this treatment of *longe* and *multo* with the superlative I am indebted
to Thielmann, *De sermonis proprietatibus quae leguntur apud Cornificium et
in primis Ciceronis libris*, p. 69 ff., and to Wölfflin, *Lateinische und romanische Comparation*, p. 37 ff.

[2] Wölfflin, *Lateinische und romanische Comparation*, pp. 39-40.

Pollio, p. 44. b) *With negative force.*[1] S. 2. 3[137] *male* tutae
mentis. 4[21] *male* creditur. 5[45], 6[67], Ep. 1. 19[3], 20[13]. For the disproportion in the number of times *male* occurs in H. and J. cf. the
remark on *bene*, p. 24.

multo, H. 7, J. 1. J. 13[196]. Where *multo* might have been
written J. sometimes uses *longe* or *multum*. See under those
words. For *multo* with the superlative see under *longe* in H. a)
and in J. (end).

multum, H. 12, J. 5. In *H.: With an adjective.* S. 2. 3[147]
multum celer. 5[92], Ep. 1. 10[3] *multum* dissimiles. 2. 2[62]. For
this usage consult Wölfflin, *Lateinische und romanische Comparation*, p. 8. It is vulgar in its origin, and frequent in Plautus.
Reisig, N. 402[a]; Krebs, II, p. 101. It occurs in Cic. Off. 1. 109,
Agr. 3. 13.

In *J.*: a) *With an adjective, as above.* 10[3] *multum* diversa.
b) *With the comparative.* 10[197] *multum* hic robustior. 12[66]. This
usage is not common, and is not found in Cicero or Caesar.[2]
Plaut. Most. 3. 2[137], Luc. 2[225], Quint. 10. 1. 94, Sil. 13[704].[3]

nequaquam, H. 2, J. 0. S. 2. 4[48], Ep. 2. 1[20].
Nequaquam is a prose word. Besides the above examples I
find in poetry only Plaut. Cas. 3. 2[1], Trin. 2. 4[16].

nequiquam, H. 2, J. 1. H. S. 2. 7[27], Ep. 1. 3[32]. J. 8[205]. *Nequi-
quam* is almost entirely avoided by silver prose-writers. Only
Quintilian and Tacitus use it once each: Quint. 8. 2. 2, Tac. Hist.
2. 24. Among silver poets Persius uses it 3 times (2[51], 4[14, 30]),
Lucan once, Valerius 14 times, Silius 22 times, Statius 16 times.
Martial does not use the word, employing *frustra* 11 times.
Wölfflin, Archiv, II, pp. 7–10.

nimis, H. 6, J. 1.[4]
nimium, H. 7, J. 0.
pariter, H. 4, J. 11. J. uses *pariter* where *simul* might be
expected. See under *simul*, p. 22. J. does not use *simul*.
parum, H. 3, J. 0.
prave, H. 4, J. 0. S. 2. 3[67] sive ego *prave* seu recte hoc volui.
Ep. 1. 1[104] *prave* sectum . . . unguem. 2. 1[266], A. P. 88 prudens
prave. Cf. *recte* and the last remarks on that word.

[1] Cf. Wilkins on Ep. 1. 19[3].
[2] Krebs, II, p. 101.
[3] For *multum ante*, *infra*, etc., consult Krebs, II, p. 101, and Kühner,
Lateinische Grammatik, II, p. 295.
[4] 6[115].

pulchre, H. 2, J. o. S. 2. 8[19] *pulchre* fuerit tibi. A. P. 428
clamabit enim, '*pulchre*, bene, recte.'

qui, H. 15, J. o. H. uses *qui* as = *quo modo* in every case,
never as = *quare*, or in any of the other uses so common in early
Latin.[1] a) *With a verb*. S. 1. 1[1] *qui* fit ... ut ... 1[108] illuc redeo
qui nemo ut avarus se probet.[2] 2. 3[108, 260]. Ep. 1. 6[44], A. P. 462.
b) *With an adjective*. S. 2. 3[241] *qui* sanior ac si ...? 3[275, 311], 7[105].
Ep. 1. 6[42], 16[63] *qui* melior servo, *qui* liberior, sit avarus ... non
video. c) *Alone*. S. 1. 3[128] sutor tamen est sapiens. *qui?* d)
In anaphora. Ep. 1. 16[63].

I find no substitute of J. for *qui*. He uses *quo ... modo* once
(6[275]). *Qui* is a prose word. I find no clear example in classical
or silver poetry beyond those in the S. and Ep. of Horace, Pers.
1[56], Phaed. 1. 1[7]. Caesar uses *qui* only B. C. 2. 32[9], Nepos only
Ar. 3. 2. In silver prose I find only Quint. 5. 13. 45, 6. 1. 7, 7. 3.
34, and Pliny, 7. 5. 189.

recte, H. 33, J. 1.[3] H. uses *recte* broadly. a) S. 1. 4[13] scribendi
recte. A. P. 309. b) S. 2. 2[106] uni nimirum tibi *recte* semper
erunt res, i. e. things will be prosperous with you. 3[162]. c) Ep.
1. 1[66] rem facias; rem si possis *recte*; si non, quocumque modo
rem. d) Ep. 1. 2[41] *recte* vivendi. 6[29], 8[1], 16[17]. e) Ep. 1. 7[3] *recte*
... valentem. 16[21]. f) Ep. 1. 8[15] ut valeat ... ut placeat iuveni
percontare: si dicet '*recte*' ... g) A. P. 428 clamabit enim 'pulchre, bene, *recte*.' The large use of *recte* in H. is partially to be
accounted for by his conversational style. So e), f), g) above.
H. uses *recte* 4 times in the Odes, whereas the word appears to
be rare elsewhere in poetry. Beyond the examples in Plautus,
Terence and H., I find only Ov. Pont. 2. 3[13], Mart. 7. 70[2], J. 9[118].

secus, H. 1, J. o. A. P. 149. Among the silver poets I find
only one example of *secus*—Luc. 10[447].

sic, H. 60, J. 26. In *H.*: a) "*As follows*," *of a direct quotation*.
S. 1. 1[65] ut quidam ... dives populi contemnere voces *sic* solitus:
populus me sibilat ... 2. 1[51], 6[79], 8[60], Ep. 1. 17[1h], 2. 2[7]. b) *Thus*,
in the above words, of a direct quotation. S. 1. 4[120]. c) *For adeo*.
S. 2. 8[3] 'ut ... iuvit te cena?' '... *sic* ut mihi numquam ...
fuerit melius.' d) *sic ... si*. Ep. 1. 7[69] *sic* ignovisse putato me

---

[1] See the dissertation of Kienitz, *De qui localis modalis apud priscos
Latinos usu* (Leipsic, 1879).
[2] Here I follow the reading of Cruquius, Palmer, Kiessling, and the last
edition of Orelli, against the formerly accepted *illuc ... redeo nemo ut*.
[3] 9[1h].

tibi, si cenas hodie mecum. e) *In adjuration.* S. 2. 3^{300} stoice, post damnum *sic* vendas omnia pluris, qua me stultitia insanire putas? For this usage see Kiessling on Od. 1. 3^1. It survived in Italian.[1] f) *sic . . . ut, for tantum . . . quantum.* S. 2. 8^{36} parochi . . . nil *sic* metuentis ut acris potiores. g) *In drawing a moral conclusion.* Ep. 1. 10^{79} *sic* qui paupertatem veritus potiore metallis libertate caret dominum vehet. Cf. Ep. 1. 9^{10}. h) *For* TAM, *limiting an adjective.* S. 1. 3^{19} nil fuit umquam *sic* impar sibi. 5^{62}, Ep. 2. 1^{179} *sic* leve, *sic* parvum est animum quod laudis avarum subruit. i) *Limiting a verbal noun.* Ep. 2. 1^{23} *sic* fautor veterum. Cf. *quondam* b) and *modo* (in J.) c). j) *In anaphora.* Ep. 1. 18^{11-12}, 2. 1^{179}.

In *J.*: a) *sic ut = on condition that.* 8^{75} sed te censeri laude tuorum Pontice noluerim *sic* ut nihil ipse futurae laudis agas. 8^{196}. Cf. *sic . . .* si, d) above. b) ergo cavebis . . . ne tu *sic* Creticus aut Camerinus. c) 13^{191} continuo *sic* collige quod . . . e) "*As follows,*" *of a direct quotation.* 14^{211}. f) *In the above words—of a direct quotation.* 15^{21}. g) *In anaphora.* 6^{229}.

The large difference in the number of times *sic* occurs in H. and J. is partially to be attributed to the fact that H. is very fond of simile, while J. uses this figure much less frequently.

sicut, H. 2, J. 6. In *J.*: a) *As for instance.* 6^{107} multa in facie deformia, *sicut* attritus galea mediisque in naribus ingens gibbus. 7^{204}. b) *Inasmuch as, since.* 15^{9x} huius . . . miserabile debet exemplum esse cibi, *sicut* modo dicta mihi gens . . . hostibus ipsis pallorem ac maciem . . . miserantibus . . . membra aliena fame lacerabant. Only two other examples of *sicut* in this sense are quoted—Plaut. Epid. 2. 2^{87} and Mil. 4. 1^{28}.[2]

tam, H. 13, J. 25. H. uses *tam* with a verb only once. Ep. 1. 7^{18} *tam* teneor dono quam si . . . J. does not so use *tam.*

Instead of *tam* with an adjective or adverb, H. uses *ita* twice,[3] *tantum* three times,[4] *adeo* four times,[5] and *sic* three times.[6] J. also uses *adeo* where *tam* might have been employed. See examples under *adeo* above.

[1] Dante, Purg. 2^{16} Cotal m' apparve, *si* ancor lo veggia, Un lume . . .

[2] Pers. 1. 3^{57} is doubtful. Tyrrell on Mil. 4. 1^{28}, after Langen, denies that *sicut* can be causal. Ribbeck, *Der echte und der unechte Juvenal*, p. 48, cites this causal use of *sicut* as pointing to the spuriousness of the Fifteenth Satire.

[3] S. 1. 1^{96}, 2. 8^{76}.   [4] S. 2. $3^{313, 317}$, 5^{60}.

[5] S. 1. 1^{13}, 7^7, Ep. 1. 1^{39}, 2. 1^{61}.   [6] S. 1. 3^{19}, 5^{60}, Ep. 2. 1^{179}.

tantum, H. 14, J. 26. In *H.: Limiting an adjective.* S. 2. 3[313]
tantum dissimilem. 3[317], 5[80]. Cf. *multum* dissimiles Ep. 1. 10[3].

In *J.*: a) 1[131] cuius ad effigiem *non tantum* meiere fas est. b)
In anaphora. 7[31].

H. uses *tantum . . . quantum* twice—S. 1. 8[17], 2. 5[80]. J. does
not use this combination. H. uses *tantum* "only" 7 times, before
its word 3 times—S. 1. 4[7] mutatis *tantum* pedibus. 2. 3[140, 306]; J.
24 times, before its word 7 times.

ut (modi), H. 7, J. o. In *H.*; a) *Interrogative.* S. 2. 5[18] *ut*
ne tegam spurco Damae latus? 8[1], Ep. 1. 3[12], 18[16]. This usage,
like the following, belongs mainly to the style of conversation.
b) *Exclamatory.* S. 2. 6[53] *ut* tu semper eris derisor! 8[62], Ep. 1.
19[19]. Instead of *ut* J. uses *quam.* 10[84] *quam* timeo victus ne
poenas exigat Aiax.

utcumque, H. o, J. 1. 10[271] exitus ille *utcumque* hominis. *Ut-*
cumque here = *at any rate, in any case.* This usage occurs first
Livy 29. 15. 1. Then Ovid, Curtius, Quintilian, Pliny the Younger,
Tacitus, and Suetonius[1] use it.[2]

valde, H. 2, J. o. Ep. 1. 9[6] videt ac novit me *valdius* ipso.
A. P. 321.

The only example of *valde* I find in poetry, other than those in
Plautus and the Epistles of Horace, are Cat. 68[17] and Mart. 3. 44[5].

velut, H. 14, J. 6. In *H.*: S. 2. 8[94] ut nihil omnino gustaremus
velut illis Canidia adflasset. *Velut* here = *velut si.* A. P. 245.

In *J.*: *For velut si.* 4[59], 6[163], 13[216], 13[224]. J. does not use *velut si.*
veluti, H. 9, J. 1.[3] In *H.*: *For velut si.* S. 2. 3[98]. Martial
uses *veluti* only once (11. 36[3]).

4. *Adverbs of Chance.*

forsan, H. o, J. 2.

forsit, H. 1, J. o. *Forsit* S. 1. 6[49] appears to be ἅπαξ λεγόμενον.[4]

forsitan, H. o, J. 6. J. uses *forsitan* with the indicative. 14[295]
hac *forsitan* ipsa nocte cadet. This construction is poetical (Ovid,
Propertius) and post-Augustan. Riemann, *Études sur Tite-Live*,
p. 292.

fortasse, H. 4, J. 5.

---

[1] Krebs, II 639.

[2] Dr., *Syntax und Stil des Tacitus*, p. 9.

[3] 11[200].

[4] This passage is quoted by Priscian, p. 1015 P. *Fors et* is now read
Verg. A. 11[50] and *forsitan* Lucr. 6[735].

fortassis, H. 2, J. o. S. 1. 4[131], 2. 7[10]. Elsewhere in poetry I find *fortassis* only Plaut. As. 2. 4[86], Bacch. 4. 4[20]. Caesar and Nepos do not use the form; Cicero in the Orations only Cluent. 144 and 201.

temere,[1] H. 6, J. o. a) *non temere, not at random, not easily.* S. 2. 2[116] non ego *temere* edi luce profesta quicquam praeter holus. Schütz here explains *non . . . temere* by *non facile.* Palmer compares οὐ ῥᾳδίως. Ep. 2. 1[120] vatis avarus non *temere* est animus. 2[13]. b) *At random, easily—without the negative.* A. P. 160 iram colligit ac ponit *temere.* This usage is found in all periods, but is rare in classical prose. Krebs, II, p. 587. As H. uses *non temere*, J. uses *haud facile.* 3[141] *haud facile* emergunt quorum virtubus obstat res angusta domi.

5. *Comparative with the force of the positive.*

ocius, H. 3, J. 4. In *H.*: S. 1. 9[9] ire modo *ocius*, interdum consistere. 2. 7[34, 117].

In *J.*: 6[148] exi *ocius* et propera. 6[416], 7[21], 14[252]. Cf. Ter. Heaut. 4. 7[4], Plaut. Curc. 2. 2[26], Caes. B. G. 5. 44, Verg. A. 5[828], Pers. 3[7] *ocius* adsit huc aliquis!

citius, H. o, J. 2. 1[125] *citius* dimitte. Mosaris? 4[134]. Cf. Ter. Hec. 3. 3[4].

6. *Doubling of Adverbs.*

iam iam, H. o, J. 1. 6[628] *iam iam* privignum occidere fas est. *Iam iam* occurs in all periods, and in prose as well as poetry. Hand, III, p. 155 ff.

longe longeque, H. 1, J. o. S. 1. 6[18] quid oportet nos facere a volgo *longe longeque* remotos. Schütz remarks in his note on this passage that *longe longeque* is good Latin. Cic. Fin. 2. 21. 68; Ov. M. 4[125]; Flor. 1. 45. 4; Gell. 14. 1. 20; Digest 4. 4. 39.[2]

unde unde, H. 1, J. o. S. 1. 3[88] qui nisi . . . nummos *unde unde* extricat, i. e. *undecumque.* As to this usage see Orelli on S. 1. 3[88].

7. *Other Adverbs.*

equidem, H. 4, J. o. Concessively, *"it is true," "to be sure."* S. 2. 1[79] *equidem* nihil hinc diffindere possum, sed tamen . . . Ep.

---

[1] As regards the length of the final *e* in *temere* see the note of Wölfflin, Archiv, IV, p. 51.

[2] Schütz cites Lucr. 3[61], but Lachmann seems right in separating the words there.

2. 1[69]. H. uses *equidem* only with the first person singular. So Terence,[1] Cicero, Caesar, Vergil, Quintilian, both the Plinys, and Tacitus. Plautus, Varro, Sallust, Persius, Lucan, Curtius, Justinus and Ausonius do not regard the supposed derivation (*ego* + *quidem*) in their use of *equidem*.[2]

I find no example of *equidem* in any poet contemporary with Juvenal. Tacitus uses the word only 5 times (Agr. 33. 14, Dial. 7. 1, 21. 1, 26. 15, An. 3. 12. 19).

haud, H. 15, J. 8. In *H.*: a) *With adverbs—in litotes.* S. 2. 2[16] *haud* ita pridem. 5[18] *haud* ita Troiae me gessi. Cf. A. P. 254 *non* ita pridem and S. 2. 6[1] *non* ita magnus. Cicero has no example of *haud ita*. Caesar, Nepos, Vergil and Livy use both *haud ita* and *non ita* (rare in Livy).[3] Ep. 1. 7[40] *haud* male. b) *With adjectives—in litotes.* S. 1. 1[35] *haud* ignara. Ep. 2. 2[12b] *haud* ignobilis. c) *With pronouns—an emphatic negative.* S. 1. 4[77] *haud* illud quaerentes num ... 2. 6[115] *haud* mihi vita est opus hac. This usage is colloquial. Ter. And. 2. 1[36] *haud* ego, 3. 2[15], Hec. 2. 3[5] *haud* pol me quidem. Plaut. Capt. 3. 4[71] *haud* istuc. d) *With a causal clause.* Ep. 1. 8[1] *haud* quia grando contuderit vitis ... sed quia ... e) *With verbs.* S. 1. 9[56] and 2. 1[17] *haud* mihi dero. 1[79] *haud* petet.

H. uses *non sine* 5 times, never *haud sine*.[4] *Haud* occurs only once in the Odes and Epodes of H. (Epod. 1[32]).

In *J.*: a) *With an adverb—in litotes.* 3[161] *haud* facile. b) *With an adjective—in litotes.* 6[1] *haud* similis. 8[19b] *haud* mira. 11[17], 13[200] *haud* impunitum. 14[136], 16[8]. c) *In an exhortation.* 7[93] *haud* tamen invideas rati quem pulpita pascunt. I cannot parallel this use of *haud.* Cf. Hand, III, p. 35.[5]

plerumque, H. 6, J. 1.[6] The silver poets seem to have avoided this word, not frequent in the Augustan poets. I find no other example than J. 11[46], Phaedr. 1. 29[1], 3. 16[2]. Where *plerumque* might have been employed, J. uses *ferme* 8[73], 13[236], *fere* 10[23], 14[173]. H. also uses *fere* in this sense.

---

[1] Jordan, *Kritische Beiträge zur Geschichte der Lat. Sprache*, p. 327 ff.

[2] Ribbeck, *Lat. Partikeln*, p. 36 ff.; Jordan, *Kritische Beiträge*, p. 314 ff.

[3] Dr. I, p. 134; Kühnast, *Liv. Syntax*, p. 350.

[4] Lucr. 2[972] *haud sine.*

[5] For a discussion of *haud* in the different Latin authors consult the dissertation of Planer, *De Haud et Haud-quaquam negationum apud scriptores Latinos usu* (Jena, 1886), and Reisig, 188 N.

[6] 11[46].

praeterea, H. 3, J. 11. Where *praeterea* might have been used H. uses, a) *insuper*. S. 2. 4⁶ᴿ *insuper* addes. b) *super*. S. 2. 7⁷⁸ adde *super*. c) *adde, adde quod*. S. 1. 1⁷¹ panis ematur, olus . . . *adde* quis . . . doleat natura negatis. 2ʳ² *adde* huc *quod* . . . 2. 2⁹⁶, 3²⁷⁵, ³²¹, 7³⁹, Ep. 1. 18⁵². J. also uses *adde* thus 12⁴⁶ *adde* et bascandas et . . ., and *adde quod* 14¹¹¹ *adde quod* hunc egregium populus putat. 15¹⁷. d) *porro*. Ep. 1. 16⁶⁵ nam qui cupiet metuet quoque, *porro* qui metuens vivet, liber mihi non erit umquam.

quidem, H. 5, J. 9. In *H.: Concessively*. Ep. 1. 9⁷ multa *quidem* dixi, cur excusatus abirem, sed timui . . . Cf. *equidem* above. In *J.: Concessively*. 2¹¹ hispida membra *quidem* . . . promittunt atrocum animum, sed . . . 2¹⁵⁹, 6¹ᴺ⁴, 8¹⁴⁹, 11⁷, 12²⁶, 15²⁷.

usque, H. 17, J. 8. In *H.*: a) *With ad*. S. 1. 1⁹⁷ ad *usque* supremum tempus. 2²⁶ inguen ad obscaenum *usque*. 3⁷, 5⁸², ⁹⁶. b) *With the name of a town*. S. 1. 6¹⁰⁵ *usque* Tarentum. c) *Of time, "continually," "ever."* S. 1. 4²⁰ *usque* laborantes dum . . . 9¹⁵, ¹⁹, 2. 1⁷⁶, 7²⁴, Ep. 1. 10²¹, 2. 2¹⁷⁰, ²⁰¹, A. P. 154, 354 si peccat idem librarius *usque*. d) S. 1. 2⁶¹ poenas dedit *usque* superque quam satis est.

In *J.*: a) *With ad, a*. 10²⁹¹ *usque* ad delicias. 13¹⁵⁸ *usque* a lucifero. b) *Without ad—as a preposition.*[1] 10¹ *usque* Auroram et Gangen. *Usque* as a preposition is post-Augustan.[2] Luc. 3²⁹⁵; Pliny 3. 5. 75 Cretam *usque*, 18. 25. 215; Just. 7. 1. 4; Stat. Th. 11ᴺ⁹; Val. Fl. 2²⁹.[3] c) *With adeo*. 3ʳ¹ *usque* adeo nihil est quod . . . 5¹²⁹, 6¹ᴺ², 10²⁰¹, 15⁸².

For a full discussion of *usque* with the accusative see Wölfflin, Archiv, IV, pp. 52–67. For "*Usque als selbständiges Adverb*," and "*Usque ad, in, sub, super, post, ante*" see Thielmann, Archiv, V, pp. 438–52, and VII, p. 103 ff., respectively.

utpote, H. 4, J. 0. S. 1. 5⁹¹ inde Rubos fessi pervenimus *utpote* longum carpentes iter. 4²¹ *utpote* pluris culpari dignos. 2. 4⁹ *utpote* res tenui sermone peractas. A. P. 206 *utpote* parvus. This use of *utpote* with a participle and adjectives, instead of the more common construction with the relative, is not usual. Nepos Hann. 2. 3 puerulo me *utpote* non amplius novem annos nato.

Utpote occurs several times in Plautus; Cat. 64⁵⁶; Nep. Hann. 2.

---

[1] Cf. the similar use of *simul* and *procul* in H.

[2] Livy 44. 5. 6 *ad* has been inserted by the editors.

[3] Other examples are quoted Dr. I, p. 598.

3; Sall. Cat. 57; Asin. Pol. apud Cic. Fam. 10. 32. 4. It is found
in Cicero's Orations only Phil. 5. 30, and Terence, Caesar, Vergil
do not use it. I find no example after H. except Prudent. Apoth.
903 C.

III.—SUBSTITUTES FOR ADVERBS.

1. *Adjectives.*

In the case of many words expressing time, place, and more
especially manner, it is sometimes most difficult to determine
whether an adjective is more natural in language or an adverb.
In such cases the Latin often employs an adjective, whereas an
adverb is regularly used in English. In a number of the examples
quoted below it is impossible to say with confidence whether
adverb or adjective would be expected. In some cases I have
been influenced by the position.

In *H.*: a) nocturno certare mero, putere *diurno* Ep. 1. 19[11], 2.
2[79], A. P. 269. *hesternis* vitiis S. 2. 2[78], 6[105]. qui *nocturnus* . . .
legerit S. 1. 3[117], 2. 6[100], Ep. 1. 19[11], 2. 2[79], A. P. 269. venit *obvius*
illi adversarius S. 1. 9[71], 2. 6[51]. *omnis* in hoc sum Ep. 1. 1[11]. haec
(voluptas) *rara* cadat S. 1. 2[40], 7[27], A. P. 259. nauta . . . stertit
. . . *supinus* S. 1. 5[19]. ibam . . . nescio quid nugarum meditans
totus in illis S. 1. 9[2], 2. 7[86]. *vespertinum*que pererro saepe forum
S. 1. 6[113], 2. 4[17], Ep. 1. 6[20].

b) qui se vixisse *beatum* dicat S. 1. 1[117], 3[142], 2. 6[96]. (redemptor)
festinat *calidus* Ep. 2. 2[72]. *candidus* imperti Ep. 1. 6[68]. vivo
carus amicis S. 1. 6[70]. quae si (Ulixes) . . . *cupidus* . . . bibisset
Ep. 1. 2[24]. mihi *dulces* ignoscent . . . amici S. 1. 3[139], 4[135]. potius
quam . . . *ferus* impingas Ep. 1. 13[x]. *gnavus* . . . pete Ep. 1. 6[20].
idoneus imperor Ep. 1. 5[21]. si quis . . . laudat . . . *ignarus* S. 2.
6[79]. (Aristius) fugit *improbus* S. 1. 9[73], 2. 6[29]. agitant pueri *in-
cautique* sequuntur A. P. 456. cur versus factitet; utrum . . . an
triste bidental moverit *incestus* A. P. 272. (ne dominus) *incom-
modus* augat Ep. 1. 18[75]. qui . . . famae servit *ineptus* S. 1. 6[16].
cur lector premat . . . *iniquus* Ep. 1. 19[36]. imperor . . . non *invi-
tus* Ep. 1. 5[22]. si possum donata reponere *laetus* Ep. 1. 7[39].
(Lucilius) cum flueret *lutulentus* S. 1. 4[11]. Varius discedit *maestus*
S. 1. 5[93]. cur . . . stringat *malus* S. 1. 2[8]. quem *miserum* . . .
vixisse S. 1. 2[21], A. P. 170. *pravus* facis S. 1. 4[79]. *probus* quis
nobiscum vivit S. 1. 3[56], 6[10]. poema qui . . . *prodigus* emit Ep. 2
1[238]. *prudens* praetereo S. 1. 10[54]. *sedulus* importes Ep. 1. 13[5].

quodsi ... *strenuus* anteis Ep. 1. 2[70], 7[71]. si quid peccaro *stultus*
S. 1. 3[140], 6[15], 2. 6[x], Ep. 1. 2[24], 14[12]. *taciturnus* pasces Ep. 1. 20[12].
tacitus aiebam S. 1. 9[12], 2. 5[6x], Ep. 2. 2[145]. quid iuvat ... te argenti
pondus ... *timidum* deponere terra? S. 1. 1[42]. pono *tristi*sque
recedo Ep. 1. 16[55]. at ille labetur in omne *volubilis* aevum Ep.
1. 2[47].

In *J.*: a) *contrarius* ire priori 9[21], 10[70]. praebebit vati *crebrum*
poppysma 6[5x4]. *fortuitus* cadat in terras ... ignis 13[225]. *hesternae*
occurere cenae 9[41], 14[129]. cuicumque (illa) est *obvia* 6[412], 8[159], 10[63].
si luditur alea *pernox* 8[10]. imputat hunc rex, et quamvis *rarum*,
tamen imputat 5[15], 8[63], 10[18], 13[8]. qui ... cubat in faciem ... *supinus* 3[280].

b) qui ... *anxius* optat 10[60]. (Hannibal) *cautus* circumagat
... cohortes 7[164]. vivite *contenti* casulis 14[170]. *improba* natos ...
reliquit 6[56]. aestuat (Alexander) *infelix* augusto limite mundi
10[169]. *iratus* cadat in terras ... ignis 13[225]. frange *miser* calamos
7[27], 10[332], 13[112], 14[64], 2[159]. (illa) cometen *prima* videt 6[506]. quod
securus ames 6[62]. ille *superbus* incedet 12[125]. *tacitus* ... recedas
3[297], 9[94]. praemia sumas *tristis* 3[57], 6[128].

2. Adverbial Phrases.

In *H.*: *aequo animo* S. 1. 5[8]. *cum risu* Ep. 2. 3[358]. *ex more*
S. 2. 3[280]. *hoc pacto* S. 2. 3[147]. *in contraria* S. 1. 2[24]. *in primis*
S. 2. 2[11]. *omni parte* S. 1. 2[34]. *pede fausto* Ep. 2. 2[57]. *pleno* ...
cornu Ep. 1. 12[29]. *post haec* Ep. 1. 8[13]. *post hoc* S. 2. 2[123], 8[31], Ep.
2. 1[175], 2[28]. *quo ... loco* Ep. 1. 12[25]. *quo ... modo* Ep. 1. 6[x].
quocunque modo Ep. 1. 1[66]. *quo pacto (quo ... pacto)* S. 1. 4[56, 90],
7[2], 8[40], 2. 4[8], 7[22], Ep. 1. 6[10], 8[13], 17[2], 2. 1[171]. *recto more* Ep. 2. 2[131].
sine sensu S. 1. 4[77]. *sinu laxo* S. 2. 3[172]. *super hoc* Ep. 2. 2[24].

In *J.*: *ad hoc* 10[137]. *dextro pede* 10[5]. *ex quo* 1[x1]. *hoc ... modo*
13[38, 73]. *in parte* 11[29]. *in praecipiti* 1[149]. *in primis* 8[121]. *omnibus
in rebus* 9[42]. *parte alia* 6[437], 7[114, 182]. *post haec* 8[247]. *post terga*
13[16]. *primo ... loco* 5[12].

INDEX, WITH NUMBER OF TIMES THE ADVERBS OCCUR.

Only words of Part II are included here, and those of Part I which show striking disproportion in the number of times they occur, or else, in case of a failure to appear in one author, where some explanation has been offered for their non-appearance.

abhinc, H. 2; p. 6.

adeo, H. 4, J. 15; p. 23.

adhuc, H. 6, J. 13: p. 15.

alias, H. 3; p. 16.

alio, H. 2; p. 7.

alioqui, H. 2; p. 24.

aliquando, J. 3; p. 16.

aliter, H. 1, J. 4; p. 24.

ante, H. 2, J. 9; pp. 6, 16.

bene, H. 43, J. 11; p. 24.

benigne, H. 3; p. 25.

brevi, H. 1; p. 16.

breviter, J. 1; p. 16.

certatim, H. 1; p. 2.

citius, J. 2; p. 31.

confestim, H. 1; p. 2.

dehinc, H. 2; pp. 6, 16.

dein, H. 2, J. 1; p. 17.

deinceps, H. 1; p. 17.

deinde, H. 3, J. 12; pp. 6, 17.

demum, H. 1; p. 17.

denique, H. 15; p. 17.

dextrorsum, H. 1; p. 3.

dudum, J. 2; p. 17.

dulce, H. 2; p. 7.

eo, H. 9; p. 7.

equidem, H. 4; p. 31.

extra, H. 1; p. 6 (cf. 7).

ferme, J. 2; p. 5.

foras, H. 2; p. 8.

foris, H. 2, J. 2; p. 8.

forsan, J. 2; p. 30.

forsit, H. 1; p. 30.

forsitan, J. 6; p. 30.

fortasse, H. 4, J. 5; p. 30.

fortassis, H. 2; p. 31.

frustra, H. 8; p. 25.

furtim, H. 5; p. 2.

grande, J. 1; p. 7.

hac, H. 2; p. 8.

hactenus, H. 2; p. 6.

haud, H. 15, J. 8; p. 32.

hic, H. 17, J. 25; p. 8.

hinc, H. 14, J. 19; p. 8.

hodie, H. 9, J. 6; p. 17.

huc, H. 9, J. 3; p. 9.

humane, H. 1; p. 25.

iam, H. 33, J. 97; p. 18.

ibi, J. 7; p. 9.

ibidem, J. 1; p. 9.

illic, H. 4, J. 17; p. 9.

illinc, H. 1, J. 4; p. 10.

illuc, H. 5, J. 3; p. 10.

inde, H. 8, J. 40; p. 10.

interea, H. 2, J. 14; p. 19.

interius, J. 1; p. 12.

intra, H. 1; pp. 6, 7.

introrsum, H. 2; p. 3.

intus, H. 7, J. 1; p. 12.

istic, H. 1, J. 1; p. 12.

istinc, H. 2, J. 1; p. 12.

ita, H. 23, J. 4; p. 25.

item, H. 2; p. 26.

longe, H. 9, J. 8; p. 26.

male, H. 28, J. 4; p. 26.

modo, H. 18, J. 19; p. 19.

multo, H. 7, J. 1; p. 27.

multum, H. 12, J. 5; p. 27.

nequaquam, H. 2; p. 27.

nequiquam, H. 2, J. 1; p. 27.

nimis, H. 6, J. 1; p. 27.

nimium, H. 7; p. 27.

nusquam, H. 4, J. 2; p. 12.

obiter, J. 2; p. 13.

ocius, H. 3, J. 4; p. 31.

olim, H. 23, J. 19; p. 19.

pariter, H. 4, J. 11; p. 27.

parum, H. 3; p. 27.

passim, H. 2; p. 13.

peregre, H. 2; p. 13.

perraro, H. 1; p. 7.

persaepe, H. 3; p. 7.

plerumque, H. 6, J. 1; p. 32.

populariter, J. 1; p. 4.

porro, H. 4, J. 4; p. 13.

post, H. 8, J. 1; pp. 6, 7, 13.

postmodo, H. 1; p. 6.

potenter, H. 1; p. 5.

praeterea, H. 3, J. 11; p. 33.

prave, H. 4; p. 27.

procul, H. 7, J. 6; p. 13.

prodigialiter, H. 1; p. 5.

prope, H. 16, J. 1; p. 14.

protinus, H. 3, J. 7; pp. 6, 20.

pulchre, H. 2; p. 28.

qua, H. 4, J. 1; p. 14.

quando, H. 17, J. 23; p. 20.

quandocumque, H. 3; pp. 4, 20.

quandoque, H. 1, J. 3; p. 20.

quandoquidem, J. 3; p. 7.

qui, H. 15; p. 28.

quidem, H. 4, J. 9; p. 33.

quo, H. 30, J. 6; p. 14.

quoad, H. 1; p. 21.

quondam, H. 7, J. 7; p. 21.

quorsum, H. 5; pp. 3, 14.

quotiens, H. 3, J. 19; p. 21.

raro, H. 4; p. 21.

recte, H. 33, J. 1; p. 28.

repente, J. 2; p. 21.

retrorsum, H. 2; p. 3.

secus, H. 1; p. 28.

semel, H. 14, J. 5; p. 21.

sic, H. 60, J. 26; p. 28.

sicut, H. 2, J. 6; p. 29.

simul, H. 27; p. 22.

singultim, H. 1; p. 2.

sinistre, H. 1; p. 5.

sinistrorsum, H. 1; p. 3.

suave, H. 1; p. 7.

subinde, H. 2; p. 6.

super, H. 3; p. 7.

superne, H. 2; p. 14.

tam, H. 13, J. 25; p. 29.

tandem, H. 7, J. 11; p. 22.

tantum, H. 14, J. 26; p. 30.

temere, H. 6; p. 31.

tributim, H. 1; p. 2.

triste, H. 1; p. 7.

tum, H. 15, J. 3; p. 23.

tunc, H. 3, J. 34; p. 23.

ubi (*loci*), H. 11, J. 16; p. 14.

ubi (*temp.*), H. 29, J. 1; p. 23.

ubicumque, H. 2, J. 1; p. 15.

ubivis, H. 1; p. 7.

unde (*inter.*), H. 13, J. 14; p. 15.

unde (*rel.*), H. 13, J. 16; p. 15.

usquam, H. 4, T. 3; p. 15.

usque, H. 17, J. 8; p. 33.

ut (*modi*), H. 7; p. 30.

ut (*temp.*), H. 10, J. 2; p. 23.

utcumque, J. 1; p. 30.

utpote, H. 4; p. 33.

utrobique, H. 1; p. 15.

valde, H. 2; p. 30.

velut, H. 14, J. 6; p. 30.

veluti, H. 9, J. 1; p. 30.

verniliter, H. 1; p. 4.

viritim, H. 1; p. 2.

www.ingramcontent.com/pod-product-compliance
Lightning Source LLC
Chambersburg PA
CBHW030911260626
47169CB00008B/2790